Gruoch Macbeth

Hero Leona

Cathérine de Val

Brabrantia

rmione Regina

/a Ophelia Polon

rtrude of Denmark

SHE
SPEAKS!

SHE
SPEAKS!

WHAT SHAKESPEARE'S
WOMEN *MIGHT*
HAVE SAID

HARRIET
WALTER

virago

VIRAGO

First published in Great Britain in 2024 by Virago Press

5 7 9 10 8 6 4

A CIP catalogue record for this book
is available from the British Library.

ISBN 978-0-349-01891-1

Typeset in Goudy by M Rules
Printed and bound in Great Britain by
Clays Ltd, Elcograf S.p.A.

Papers used by Virago are from well-managed forests
and other responsible sources.

Virago Press
An imprint of
Little, Brown Book Group
Carmelite House
50 Victoria Embankment
London EC4Y 0DZ

The authorised representative
in the EEA is
Hachette Ireland
8 Castlecourt Centre
Dublin 15, D15 XTP3, Ireland
(email: info@hbgi.ie)

An Hachette UK Company
www.hachette.co.uk

www.virago.co.uk

To so many unheard women's voices and to one special Guy

She speaks: O, speak again!

Romeo and Juliet

Do you not know I am a woman? When I think, I
must speak.

As You Like It

VIOLA:

My father had a daughter loved a man,
As it might be, perhaps, were I a woman,
I should your lordship.

DUKE ORSINO:

And what's her history?

VIOLA:

A blank, my lord. She never told her love.

Twelfth Night

Contents

Introduction

If I could time travel, I would go back to London in the 1590s and early 1600s to see one of Shakespeare's plays performed by the Lord Chamberlain's Men or the King's Men. I am bursting with curiosity to know how they acted in those days and, most especially, since actresses weren't allowed on the stage for another half century or so, to see how boys and young men portrayed Rosalind, Mistress Quickly, Cleopatra or Lady Macbeth.

Theatre was a relatively new art form to the citizens of London and the city itself was a small place, so the pool of boy actors Shakespeare could draw on wouldn't have been made up of future Laurence Oliviers and Ian McKellens. For the most part they were probably quite shouty and unsubtle schoolboys, pulling faces and hamming it up. Hamlet's advice to the travelling players not to 'saw the air too much' or 'tear a passion to tatters' gives one a bit of a clue as to what Shakespeare himself warned his company against. But he was also aware that high art would be 'caviar to the general' and that an average contemporary audience wouldn't be too concerned about the nuances of acting. It was enough to be in the buzzy atmosphere of a playhouse, being told an exciting story.

This is all speculation. Frustratingly, we will never know the truth. Theatre is an art form that by its very nature insists 'you had to *be* there'.

I once read that a young male player would be expected 'to have a command of rhetoric, to speak well, have good facial expressions and an aliveness of movement'. So I suspect that acting in those days owed more to expert mimicry and physical posturing than anything close to the interiority and authenticity the modern actor is expected to bring to the stage. Did a boy player ask 'What's my motivation?' or have to dredge up some Method-like emotional memory in order to play a part? I rather doubt it.

In the small window between recruitment at about age ten and first beard growth (later than nowadays, so around eighteen), a young actor could become an expert in his field and play girls and women *outwardly* very convincingly. What they couldn't do was speak from the experience of *being* a girl or a woman.

They would never say to Shakespeare, 'I think Gertrude needs to answer back here', or 'Can you give me a bit more of a speech about what Lady Capulet feels about her daughter dying?', or 'Can you explain why Lear's daughters Goneril and Regan are so hateful?'

In this book I have had the temerity to invent some answers to some of these and other questions that the modern actress – and a modern audience – might wish to ask.

I worship Shakespeare and feel very irreverent, shamelessly piggy-backing on his giant shoulders. His psychological insight is second to none. His language is miraculous. His daring with forms and his coinage of some two thousand new words make him a great experimenter. He held 'the mirror up to Nature' as no one else before or since. But ... being a sixteenth-century man his mirror sometimes gives only a sliver of reflection of women and women's lives. It is a beautiful sliver but limited in scope.

If Shakespeare wasn't the Poet for All Time whose truths are held to be eternal, this wouldn't be too much of a problem, but many of his characters have become almost immortal. Perhaps the most universally famous character in fiction is Hamlet. He has come to represent Everyman. He is the great articulator of the human condition and women as well as men are accustomed to identifying with this Danish prince from a very different time. If we were to swap things round, would men similarly identify with a female character as representative of all humankind?

These are some of the thoughts I had as I pondered the long shadow of Shakespeare's genius and tried to think of ways to let a little sunlight in on some of his women's stories. I like to think he wouldn't mind.

I haven't tried to imitate him or write in cod Elizabethan language, but I have found a natural and helpful structure in the iambic pentameter – five di-*dums* to a line (with the occasional trochaic *dum*-di) – that he used. Paradoxically, I found it easier to write in rhyming couplets or sonnet form than in blank verse (the same number of di-*dums*, but without the rhymes) because that suddenly looks like serious poetry and leaves my choice of words more exposed somehow. Shakespeare frequently broke his own rules of rhythm and rhyme, but he can get away with it because of the depth of his poetic thinking and dramaturgy.

A large part of the enjoyment of the writing was to find out how much I have absorbed of Shakespeare's rhythms and imagery simply by dint of having played twenty-one (yes, I counted) of his roles. These characters *exist* in the framework of the verse. The pulse of their thoughts is laced through their speeches and over five decades of internally listening to them and then speaking those lines out loud, I was excited to find how naturally these invented verses came to me.

Do speak them aloud – if you like that sort of thing. I hope you will enjoy that, and also enjoy being tantalised by the odd phrase or echo that reminds you of some famous line of the Bard's. These don't usually come from the play I am dealing with in that chapter: my women borrow from one another and toss imagery between them.

Just as when playing a classical part I try to build a bridge between myself and the character and form a kind of hybrid (a sort of Harriet Macbeth, or whatever), in the same way I have written these speeches in a contemporary language while hoping to remain in character. Some are tragical, some comical, tragical-historical, farcical-historical. Most speak alone but sometimes I bring together women from different plays so they can share and compare their stories.

I was alerted to a list (available on Shakespeareswords.com) of every Shakespeare role ranked by the numbers of lines they speak, from Hamlet, who has the most, to some poor guy called Herbert who only has one line in *Richard III*. On that list, Rosalind from *As You Like It* is the longest female role but she is only at number fifteen. Tellingly, there are only fifteen women's roles listed in the top one hundred (Lady Macbeth is way down at number 138, which makes her lasting impact all the more surprising). In making my choices of who to give voice to, I have tended to focus more on those who don't get much of a look in or are rather misunderstood than on those to whom Shakespeare has already given a lot to say.

I have also included a few characters that seem to me very gender fluid, and I like to think that Shakespeare, who in his casting could switch a boy to a woman and back again, and play with all the ambiguity in between, would understand.

KATE

The Taming of the Shrew

Most people now agree that this is a pretty impossible play to stomach in this day and age, being as it is a 'comedy' about a 'shrewish' woman who comes to know her place 'beneath your husband's foot'. Hard though it is, we have to admit that Shakespeare probably did mean it to be funny, and that if we try to bend it into a more po-faced feminist, or ironic, shape it doesn't really stand up. We just want a different play. I don't want to doom it or say it can never be played again, because I am reverent enough of the Bard to think none of his words should be buried, and I have seen a couple of productions that convinced me either by means of a blanket sarcasm or of a quirk of casting – whereby Kate seemed genuinely changed by the sheer charisma of her Petruchio and he in turn seemed humbled by her. The trouble was that my immediate conviction evaporated fairly soon.

I was never invited to play her, and I pity the poor actor who has to find their way through Kate's last capitulatory speech at the wedding, having put up with Petruchio's verbal and physical abuse over all the previous scenes. The actor's responsibility is threefold: to keep the comedy buoyant for some of the audience; appease other members of the audience who don't want Kate to give in; and then there is a kind of duty to the whole of womankind to persuade them that the play does not defend male bullying and domestic abuse. Impossible!

I have my editor Lennie Goodings to thank for the title of this next piece. At one point I moved it on to *The Turn of the Shrew* (à la Henry James) but that was probably a pun too far. In any case, I make no apologies for this reclamation of the character. I want to give Kate her turn to say what she really wants to say, not just to the guests at the onstage banquet but also to the audience in the stalls.

The Turning of the Shrew

What! Did you pay to come and laugh at me?
To see a woman scorned, abused and maimed?
Abducted, tortured, starved? Is that a comedy?
Do you delight to see her spirit tamed?
You men, I maybe get it, but you wives!
Whose side are *you* on, ladies? Don't you see?
This is the stuff of many women's lives,
Not limited to brawling broads like me.
Would you prefer to be my sister Bianca,
Who's always been the pretty goody two-shoes.
You think she's happy wedded to that wanker?
You think that sweetheart has no anger issues?
Your men don't give a toss how good or bad you are:
They know that goods and chattels cannot choose.
I'm not the only 'harridan' in Padua
Whose husband knows just where to hide a bruise.
Petruchio supposed he could seduce me,
Could break me on his wheel to win a bet,
By mixing cruelty with charm thought to reduce me
To a willing snivelling slaving nervous wreck.
But I who pride myself on bold defiance
Broke plates in answer to his mockery.
Refusing him the gift of my compliance
I had no choice but throw *more* crockery.
Protected in the crowded theatre pit
You roar with laughter at this slapstick 'play',
You join the rabble as they jeer and spit
'Cause baiting Kate keeps your own fears at bay.
You say, 'She must enjoy it, or she'd run.

She's got some spunk, she'd never let him win.
His seeming cruelty is all in fun.'
You will not see the truth that I'm all-in.
Then, what relief, what comfort come the wedding!
'She loved him all along, the truth shines through.
With acquiescent grace she does his bidding.
She smiles, you see? He's truly tamed the shrew.'
Admit it, ladies, marriage is a farce,
A power game that holy law allows.
Know that your lord and master is an arse
And tie the knot with firmly knitted brows.
At curtain down it's once more to the breech:
Go to it, wives! – the war this shrew enshrines.
If men believe my last repentant speech,
They haven't learned to read between the lines.

GERTRUDE I

Hamlet

played Ophelia in 1980 at the Royal Court in Sloane Square, London. Jonathan Pryce was the extraordinary edgy Hamlet and it was directed by Richard Eyre. The brief at the Royal Court at that time was to give new writing the stature of the classics and classic works a contemporary spin. With its secular take on ghosts and notions of heaven, hell and purgatory, and its atmosphere of an oppressive political state, our production fulfilled that brief and was dubbed 'The *Hamlet* of the 80s'. It may seem nothing new now, but it was a breakthrough production and a natural progression for me from the political fringe into the 'legit' London theatre scene. I was daunted by the starry company I was in (besides Jonathan, there was Jill Bennett playing Gertrude and Michael Elphick as Claudius, and the poet Christopher Logue writing his own speech as the Player King), but I loved playing the part. Ophelia gets to express all her anger and bewilderment, and her broken heart in the outlet that is her 'mad scene'. Not so poor Gertrude.

Gertrude has no such release when Hamlet harangues her in her chamber and asks how she could possibly love Claudius after having been with his father, whom Hamlet blindly hero-worships. He then tells her that her love for Claudius can't possibly be sexual because

... at your age
The hey-day in the blood is tame, it's humble,
And waits upon the judgment:

She just has to sit there and take it. OK, she gnashes and wails a bit, but we never get her defence or her explanation. The audience has been carefully primed to take Hamlet's side in all things.

Learning that our parents are flawed and allowing them their flaws is part of the process of growing up, but parents continue to be blamed for so much in our lives and mothers are usually less forgiven than fathers. Perhaps it is because, on the whole, fathers are *expected* to be judgemental and stern, so we worship them for any moments of kindness or attention they bestow on us. Mothers, on the other hand, get a much rougher deal. From our infancy we expect them to feed us and instantly to attend to our every need. If they withdraw from us or hold anything back we wail and scream until we get what we want. While this is necessary when we are helpless infants, it can become a lasting habit to expect this unconditional love and renunciation of the self from our mothers. God forbid they should have a life of their own, least of all a sex life.

Given this context, Hamlet's attitude to Gertrude seems all too familiar.

Watching this scene from the wings each night, I remember that I longed for Gertrude to answer back and defend herself.

What Gertrude *Wanted* to Say

Oh Hamlet, if you only understood
Your damnèd dad was anything but good.
He was a viper when he went to school.
At home he rampaged like a shackled bull,
Spoiling for wars that meddled with his mind
And made him *more* despotic and unkind.
He took his violent rages out on me,
Who sheltered you from all this agony.
So you grew up believing him a saint
And I could never say, 'A saint he ain't.'
Admit you rarely saw him. After all,
He oft was busy with some foreign brawl.

Your uncle was my only comforting.
We'd been in love from childhood, but the King
(The old King, your old grandad) and his mare
Insisted that I wed their precious heir.
A marriage of convenience, you see,
But deeply *in*convenient for me.
Much more than that, it broke your uncle's heart
That we were forced to live our lives apart.

And now you tell me of this fratricide;
He told me 'natural causes', but he lied.
I see now our unseemly bed was cursed;
I understand you now. So do your worst.

Yet . . . though I know that what he did was wrong,
Perhaps he hoped the poison was so strong
It painlessly would send the King to sleep,
Leaving no time for counting woolly sheep
But straight knit up the ravelled sleeve of care?
Then we'd be free to wander everywhere
Overtly loving, spend whole days in bed,
Surfeiting those appetites so long unfed.
(You're wrong to think that sex begins to pall:
The blood at our age has not cooled at all.)

Your father's ghost torments us even now.
My love for Claud has withered on the bough.
You've hurt Ophelia's feelings and you've changed.
I don't believe you really are deranged,
Just playing for time till everything's aligned.
But knowing you, you won't make up your mind
Until the court is poisoned, every one.
Including you, my fallen sparrow son.
But break my heart for Will has held my tongue.

ROSALIND

As You Like It

Like any resident playwright, Shakespeare would have written to the strengths of his acting company, and aside from the fact they are fewer and usually shorter, his major female roles are as rich and complex as his males. This, and the law of averages, tells me there must have been a handful of stand-out gifted boy players in circulation in Shakespeare's London.

One such player whose name we know was Alexander Cooke. It is thought that he was the first Rosalind. Did some *je ne sais quoi* about this boy strike Shakespeare and inspire him to create one of his most wonderful female parts?

Shakespeare incorporated into *As You Like It* the fact that the actor was 'more than common tall' and used it again to comedic effect in *A Midsummer Night's Dream* when he pitted the 'painted maypole' Helena against the 'dwarf . . . acorn . . . burr' Hermia. The probable line of parts for Cooke would have been Rosalind, Helena, Viola, Portia, while Celia, Hermia, Maria and Nerissa were all played by a smaller lad.

In writing the part of Rosalind, Shakespeare had very likely seen in Cooke not only the skill and charm to make men and women fall in love with him but also the wit and versatility to keep the audience interested and drive the action of the play as only a handful of his female roles do. I like to think we modern actresses can thank this collaboration of playwright and actor for the chance to occasionally run the show.

I was offered the part of Rosalind a couple of times but for various reasons I couldn't take it up. However, I have played many of Shakespeare's longer parts – Cleopatra, Imogen, Portia in *The Merchant of Venice* – and in those roles I got a taste of the mental and physical energy it takes to motor large chunks of a Shakespeare play. It is a rare experience for a woman. You seldom see us sweating at the curtain call.

If women actors owe a debt to Alexander Cooke and his ilk for the sexual sophistication and emotional range that Shakespeare saw and developed in them, on the negative side, we perhaps have to blame their adolescence for our short lives in the repertoire. A boy's career playing women was transitory. Once he started to grow facial hair his girl-playing days were numbered, and he would graduate to the male roles or perhaps drop out altogether.

Flute in *A Midsummer Night's Dream* protests:

Nay, faith, let me not play a woman; I have a beard coming.

To which Quince replies:

That's all one: you shall play it in a mask, and you may speak as small as you will.

Malvolio in *Twelfth Night* describes Viola/Cesario as:

Not yet old enough for a man, nor young enough for a boy; as a squash is before 'tis a peascod, or a codling when 'tis almost an apple.

There is something very poignant about a performer on the cusp of manhood. When I hear a boy soprano, I feel a sadness for a vanishing moment in time. Many don't make the transition to tenor or baritone, or if they do, they may never be so special again. That pure voice of their childhood has, as in Prospero's words, 'melted into air, into thin air'.

All of this militates against the modern female actress developing a lifetime's work through a line of parts in the classics. Her male counterparts can progress from Romeo and Hamlet to Macbeth and King Lear, while if we are lucky we get to Cleopatra (in real life thirty-nine when she died) and kind of fall of the cliff.

Yes, it is now accepted for us to play the male roles in Shakespeare, and that is wonderful, but it doesn't cover the lack of representation of older women, wives and mothers in the classical repertoire.

There is another paradoxical debt I owe to these boy players. When 'disguised' as a boy, a female character was liberated into a directness of speech and given licence for sexual innuendo. If women had been allowed to act on stage, Shakespeare might have written very differently for them. Always aware of what pleased his audience, he might have limited the female parts even more, making them less knowing and less bold for reasons of social decorum.

In this next piece, a boy Rosalind complains of his short career and makes sure we modern Shakespearean actresses pay homage to his talent.

A Boy Player Reminisces

He said 'twas not the fashion for a girl
To speak the epilogue or lead the play.
Adhering to the mores of his world,
The women in his plays had less to say.
But showman Will knew how to tantalise
And satisfy a certain urge in us:
If boys play girls, he thought, why not devise
Some leading roles that are androgynous?
One sweet young codling player then was ripe
To flaunt his talent and was up to speed
On how to use his wit and reedy pipe.
He was the perfect gamine Ganymede.

I was that boy apprenticed to my seniors
Who taught me all I knew of thespian tricks.
But once mature there followed many lean years
And my career was through at twenty-six.
But I can always say with deepest pride
Will wrote those roles for me, I paved the way.
By sheer mimetic skill I turned the tide
So all you girls can play the roles today.

THE THREE
WITCHES

Macbeth

There was a real fear of witches at the time that *Macbeth* was first performed in the early seventeenth century. The king, James I, totally believed in them, and it is well documented that the pervading fear of single or old women led to horrendous persecutions, witch hunts, hangings and burnings. Maybe even to say the word 'witch' on stage was dangerous and might invite visitations or the bad luck that the play is famous for. Macbeth refers to them as the Weird Sisters, never witches; the actual word is used only once in the play, by one of the Weird Sisters herself in reported speech: '"Aroint thee, witch!" the rump-fed ronyon cries.'

I have never played one of the Witches (apart from in those monotonic schoolgirl chants of 'Double, double toil and trouble' round the classroom, which did nothing to entice me towards Shakespeare or acting) and it is always problematic to place the Witches in the context of a modern production, so I have chosen to approach them from another point of view.

In classical drama there are few, if any, examples of old female characters, and those few are usually grotesques to be feared or ridiculed. I am sure you can come back at me with some examples of sweet, wise old ladies, and I will agree about the Countess of Roussillon in *All's Well That Ends Well*, who remembers exactly what it felt like to be young and in love and can therefore still connect with Helena. But too often the old female character is used as the immoveable obstacle to the irrepressible force of young love, or to change itself.

So unacceptable was the physical deterioration of women, even after Charles II's restoration, when women were first allowed on the stage, that most of the time older women continued to be played by men and would justify Banquo's remark when he first meets the Weird Sisters:

> ... you should be women,
> And yet your beards forbid me to interpret
> That you are so.

I also wonder whether the first actresses chose to leave what was deemed a rather dodgy profession for women and settle down into a respectable marriage with some rich admirer in the audience – yet another factor to blame for the narrow age range of an actress's career.

From my current vantage point of *being* old (yes, let's embrace the 'O' word) I feel myself to be the child, the young woman, the middle-aged and the old versions of me all wrapped into one and I hope I am still growing and learning and remaining open to change. So I used these 'Weird Sisters' to illustrate how, behind the alienating signs of age, there are sentient people who have a lot to teach us about enduring and accommodating old age. I wanted them to speak to every generation over every century, in defence of old women and of old age in general. As they say, the choice is clear: you either die too young or you will grow old.

The Witches' Rap

Or Reclaiming the 'O' Word

Whiskers, wrinkles, bags that wobble . . .
Hags in rags with legs that hobble,
Chins are double, pricked with stubble,
Brains befuddled, minds a-muddle
Living in our babbling bubble
Blamed for every trial and trouble
When all we are is OLD.

With slimy noses, grimy toeses
We're the thorns in lovely roses,
The door of hope that quickly closes.
We're prose, while poetry that flows is
Dammed by us. What our kind knows is
Every lovely thing that grows is
Destined to grow OLD.

Ostracised and criticised,
Terrorised for being wise,
Men act our parts – but in disguise,
With hooded heads and leopard eyes
Lest ugly truth should jeopardise
The myth that beauty never dies –
But look at us: we're OLD.

Old women seem the enemy,
Voracious vile and venomy,
A hideous hegemony
Of hexes and disharmony.

Unsexy, past it, pale and wizened,
We're everything a young girl isn't.
But we weren't always OLD.

Our memories are quiet wells,
Deep rich waters, echoing bells,
Love tokens, smiles and summer smells,
Our minds expanding in their shells,
Our brains protective citadels
Not almanacs for casting spells:
We're like you but just OLD.

The oak tree wears its outer coat
With pride, shows off each gnarly knot,
Each grasping root, each liver spot.
Young saplings grow from mulching rot
Of elders' bark and owe a lot
To ancestors beneath their plot,
They don't despise the OLD.

'Tis better far that you befriend
The signs foreshadowing your end.
Know that your back will surely bend,
That certain breaks will never mend,
Your voice may squeak, your breath offend.
Embrace all this if you intend
To treasure every day you spend.
Unless you die too young, my friend,
One day you will be OLD.

MISTRESS QUICKLY

Henry IV parts I and II, Henry V,
The Merry Wives of Windsor

M istress Quickly is unique in that she appears in four plays, but her character is not totally consistent within them. In the first two she is the gullible stooge to Sir John Falstaff's con tricks. She laughs devotedly at all his jokes even though he shows her little genuine affection or respect and treats her quite cruelly at times. If she cracks a joke, it is usually unwittingly. In part II of the *Henry IV* plays we see her in thrall to the madcap Pistol, an appropriately named intermittent lover who comes and goes as he pleases. Although Mistress Q is very capable of scolding him it is always good-humouredly and deep down she would forgive him everything in exchange for a squeeze or a kiss.

By *Henry V* she and Pistol have tied the knot and war brings a certain seriousness to life in the pub at Cheapside. Under this darker cloud, Mistress Quickly's dear old friend Falstaff dies. Her description of his death is one of the most touching and intimate scenes in the canon (recited by many a drama student at auditions). I had forgotten until writing this that I actually played Mistress Quickly in a Cambridge student production when I was eighteen. I seem to remember a nightclub spotlight on me while I played a few notes on a saxophone . . . well, we were students . . . it was experimental . . . sorry.

But that same saxophonist had to switch moods and describe how Falstaff on his deathbed 'Babbled o' green fields' and ended up with all his body parts 'as cold as any stone' (she'd tested them

under the sheets). Her generosity of spirit placed the old rogue
firmly 'in Arthur's bosom' – meaning he was with the Lord in
heaven.

Due to the popularity of the Cheapside characters, Queen
Elizabeth herself asked Shakespeare for an encore, so Falstaff,
Mistress Quickly and the gang were resurrected for *The Merry
Wives of Windsor* – a very silly but enjoyable play in which the
mercurial Mistress Quickly changes again to become a sort of
Puck-like agent of mischief helping the Merry Wives to get their
revenge on the predatory old fart Falstaff.

I wanted to keep Mistress Quickly alive, so I have tried to
resurrect her as a kind of eternal character that we might meet
any day in twenty-first-century London. Because she speaks in
prose most of the time in the plays, I have tried a bit of that
here. Shakespeare writes her dialogue colloquially and many of
the expressions used in the Boar's Head (the pub where Falstaff,
Prince Hal and co. hang out) can be hard for a modern audience
to fathom, being so current and topical to Shakespeare's time,
so to attempt some kind of equivalent I may have gone a bit
overboard with Mistress Q's dropped aitches and malapropisms.
I hope she will forgive me.

Alive and Kicking

Ooh goodness! How long 'ave I been around? Cencheries! Four 'undred years and more. Still in Cheapside – well, not sa cheap nowadays. It's the rich young 'ooligans that come in 'ere, hactin' like they own the place. Don't impress *me*. Not when I've 'ad the heir to the flipping throne in my ... Well, not *'ad* exackly, but 'e'd give me a friendly cuddle when 'e was in the mood. Couldn't resist him ... Well, I mean I *did* resist him, not that 'e ever ... Well, no, I LOVED THAT BOY. We all did ... and then that dreadful day. 'E broke Fat Jack's heart ...

'I know thee not, old man.' I was there. We all were. Never forget it. We 'ad to pick the poor fat fella up off the cobbles (talk abart movin' mountains), 'ad to try and patch up 'is 'eart, though it never really mended. Mind you, all these cencheries later and seems royal princes make a habit of denying they know certain people, even to this day. I'm sure you know to hoom I am referrin' to. Say na more.

Nah! You'd be surprised how little the clineteel 'as changed over the cencheries. There's Sir Francis Fullfat – 'igh up in the Parlyment 'e is. A Stablishment figure wot can break all the rules. Arrogant rogue and a Nanarchist at 'eart. Remind you of anyone? Thinks he can twist me round his fat little finger like old Jack used to, but he ain't got the charm.

Then there's Dotty Doll – her type crops up every genera- tion. Beautiful but not much up top, if you know what I mean. Shaped like an 'ourglass but her brains runs out like the sand at 'er waist ... Now I'm mixin' me metronomes but you get the gist.

We still get the red-nosed Bardolphs, usually sat sittin' in an 'armless daze in the corner, and the odd Bard, and the bad'uns, the 'ell raisers. I always 'ad a weakness for the bad boys. That

Captain Pistol gave me a run for me money. He knew he could play me cos he knew I'd a married him like a shot. (See what I did there?) Course, I got 'im in the end when 'e was too clapped out to run around any more. But 'e died on me a long while ago and I bin on me own ever since. Couldn't replace 'im even if I wanted to. Any Pistol I meet of my own age these days takes a long while to re-load, if you know what I mean.

What *is* a bit new is the young posh women who come in here on their own. I like that. Some of 'em even go on the game to make a bit of money to help get through their headucation, or raise a family on their own. Some of 'em fink they can tell us all what's what. Take that Kate Hothouse, for example, always on a rant about somefink. Only last night I 'eard her 'aranguin' some poor soldier lads – 'Oh yet for God's sake go not to these wars!' As if they 'ad a choice. Cannon fodder, bless their silly 'earts. Yeah, she's a gorgeous girl but she won't stay the course. It's a means to an end with 'er.

I turn a blind ear to them gels who 'ang around 'ere pickin' up 'clients', they call 'em now. All very business-like. But I do interfere if I see any bullying or humilification. I tell 'em we women should hang on to our pride, and I tell 'em if anyone tries anyfink on that they don't want to do, they know Quickly will live up to 'er name and chase that sort orf the premises quick as a flashin' blade.

These blokes what blame a girl for the way she dresses. I tell my girls, 'You dress how you like and if the blokes can't take it then it's them as has to change, not you.'

Mind you, I'd love there to come a day when there's no need for any of this business. When all types can get what they want in the bedroom or wherever by *asking* with respec' and no shame. But now I'm doin' misself out of a job, in'I?

I don't see myself retiring as long as I can stand and pull a pint. I like the company and who knows, we might get another Will (or Willa) Shakespeare who'll put me in their play.

Be 'ard to match old Will, of course. Oh I did love him. Fancied 'im rotten if the truth be known. I was proud to be in 'is plays, even though he took the piss out of me. Called me Quickly and then made out that I was anythink but sparky up top. S'pose it made for better laughs. Them playwriters always do alter the troof to fit their story. But I will say over the cencheries I've got wise to a thing or two. 'E might write me differently now. For a start I've learned me alphabet . . . LGBT join the Q, I say.

Whatever wags your tail. You 'ave to move with the times, don't you?

CLEOPATRA

Antony and Cleopatra

Cleopatra is considered to be the pinnacle of all female Shakespeare roles and yet, though I adored playing her, I didn't like her very much. Until she (and the actor) is tested by the grand tragedy of the final act, she seems merely skittish, egotistic and luscious. The actor playing her has the extra burden of having to convince an audience that a hard-headed Roman general would lose his strategic and political sense on account of her irresistible sexual allure.

The real Cleopatra had more in common with Elizabeth I than Shakespeare perhaps wanted to expose. Both were raised without a mother (Anne Boleyn was executed when Elizabeth was two and Cleopatra's mother is absent from any records of her upbringing). Both were clever, highly educated women who learned early how to survive in a terrifying, treacherous, very male environment in which family was no guarantee of protection – and in fact often the source of danger. Elizabeth was under constant threat from Catholic factions supporting either her sister Mary Tudor's or her cousin Mary Stuart's supposedly superior claim to the throne and Cleopatra was fighting to keep her fragile hold on her corner of the Roman Empire, which she did remarkably well until the end.

I was always so much more interested in the real Cleopatra, the politician, than in her legendary attraction for men, to the extent that the part wasn't top of my list of those I wanted to play ... until ... in 2006 I was invited by Gregory Doran to play her opposite Patrick Stewart as Antony at the RSC. Then I totally surrendered to her sexual energy, her trickery, her fun and her ultimate tragic grandeur.

Both she and Antony are narcissistically aware of their own importance on the world stage and even beyond it. When Antony believes Cleopatra is dead and is about to kill himself to be alongside her, he says,

> My queen ... Stay for me:
> Where souls do couch on flowers, we'll hand in hand,
> And with our sprightly port make the ghosts gaze:
> Dido and her Aeneas shall want troops,
> And all the haunt be ours.

(Which invariably made me shed a tear backstage.)
When it is her turn to die, Cleopatra says:

> Methinks I hear
> Antony call; I see him rouse himself
> To praise my noble act; I hear him mock
> The luck of Caesar, which the gods give men
> To excuse their after wrath: husband, I come:
> Now to that name my courage prove my title!
> I am fire and air; my other elements
> I give to baser life.

The assumption is that their lives are consequential, and that the gods are closely related to them and care deeply about both of them.

Cleopatra is aware enough of her historical importance to envisage 'Some squeaking Cleopatra boy my greatness i' the posture of a whore' in plays after her death. She longs for immortality, but not this kind. In fact, in this next piece she finds out that immortality is not all it's cracked up to be. Cleopatra – who loved being the centre of the universe – is now bored by eternity and having Antony by her side 24/7, unattended by servants, indeed not watched by anyone and thoroughly disappointed by heaven.

Another Dreary Day in Heaven

How tedious this eternity can be
In close proximity with Antony.
Who once crossed mighty oceans in his stride
Now curls up safe and cosy by my side.
In life I longed for him but now . . . ho hum.
As Cressid rightly said, 'Things won are done.'
What's love bereft of parting's sweetest sorrow,
Without the fear of losing him tomorrow?
My asp bite and his wounds are long since healed
And all our fruits and grapes come ready-peeled.
Without command and sway and sexual sizzle
It's all one dreary democratic drizzle.
This endless flowing cloudscape is so bland,
My monument has crumbled into sand.
Death killed my rule but not my self-regard:
Without an audience I find life hard.
I miss the thrill of being centre stage,
Where slaves and emp'rors cowered at my rage,
Where Nature's peaks and troughs, its fires and floods,
Reflected all the grandeur of my moods.
Now from my cloudy cushion I survey
Earth's pygmy players acting out a play
In which I am portrayed as sly and wilful,
Not as I was, politically skilful.
As I predicted, squeaking Cleopatras
Parade my shame, with shambling hammy partners
Pretending to be Antony, and fail
To match our mythic stature and our scale.
My pride and reputation are at stake –

It took some guts to suckle that damned snake.
I cannot bear to watch as wanton boys
Belittle my brave death with bendy toys.
This Mr William Shakespeare, who is he
That he will dare to make a fool of me?

CHARMIAN

Antony and Cleopatra

Charmian is Cleopatra's main handmaiden. She knows Cleopatra inside out, just as a Victorian lady's maid or even an actor's dresser might be privy to all sorts of aspects and personal habits that the person they look after would never show to anyone else. Servants to grand families witnessed domestic rows between their employers, or top-secret conversations with politicians who came to stay, and these servants were either so overlooked as human beings that no one thought to be discreet in front of them or they were arrogantly presumed to be loyal. The same is most likely the case for Cleopatra and Charmian. It doesn't occur to Cleopatra that Charmian might have a malicious longing to divulge all her mistress's secrets and that she might not be the bestie she purports to be.

There is a parallel in the theatrical version in that the actor playing Charmian (and often understudying Cleopatra) might be harbouring God knows what thoughts about the actor playing Cleopatra.

Did my Charmian (Golda Rosheuvel) perhaps think like this?

Charmian Disses her Mistress

Like snakes we circle that great narcissist
The Empress Cleopatra, and assist
Her self-deception and her vanity,
And save her from incipient insanity.
My sister Iras and the eunuch Mardian,
That ever-patient, ever-watchful guardian,
Slough off the insults from our mistress's wrath,
And stir sweet ass's milk into her bath,
Polish her silken skin with servile smiles –
Thus *we* beguile that serpent of Old Nile.
With silent signs we say, 'This whole thing stinks,'
And whisper blasphemy: 'Our quean's* no sphinx.
No mystery to us, this prima donna,'
While placing some flash headdress thing upon her.
So what if now and then her slippery tongue
Does flatter or amuse us? We're still stung
By her sweet tyranny and charming hurt.
We fear the worst when she begins to flirt:
She brought great Julius Caesar to his knees
And pricked Marc Antony with every tease.
That tired old trick, the burnished barge of gold,
Came out again and straight his heart was sold.
And who d'you think prepared that gorgeous float?
Why us, her slaves! Our wages? Half a groat.
Without us she'd be lost. It's just not fair. Oh,
Why can't I resist this female pharaoh?
Now that she's cornered, beaten and forlorn
I pity her and foolishly have sworn
To help her outwit Caesar with her death,

So she escapes and we poor saps are left
As loot for Roman soldiers on the make.
Well bugger that! Let's follow in her wake.
If she insists we never leave her side
We'll triumph with a triple suicide.

---

* A pun Shakespeare himself used, *quean* meaning prostitute/floozy/jezebel.

HERO

Much Ado About Nothing

Hero is the highest-status female in Leonato's household, where the play takes place, but her cousin Beatrice is actually the heroine of the play. Beatrice is a poor relation, not exactly a servant, who helps out and manages things around the house. Conventionally, servants were part of the subplot but in *Much Ado* it is Beatrice's relationship with her on/off lover Benedick that takes centre stage. What's wonderful is the profound sisterly love between the two women, and indeed, Shakespeare gives us two really fun women-only scenes where Hero comes into her own and takes charge of things as the leader of the household.

Claudio, Benedick's friend and fellow soldier, has fallen in love with Hero at first sight (as so many young people do in plays of the time), and they are to be married. The night before the wedding, thanks to a plot devised by the villainous Don John, Claudio witnesses two servants snogging at a window and is duped into believing the girl is his betrothed. On the strength of this very flimsy evidence, Claudio publicly rejects Hero at the altar the next day. Even Leonato is willing to believe this trumped-up story rather than trust the daughter he has known all her life.

Beatrice is furious about all this, and when Benedick, having finally declared his love, asks her to 'bid me do anything for thee', she instantly blurts out 'Kill Claudio.' Any actor playing Beatrice has to ask themselves whether this is a mad impulse that she doesn't really mean, or does she mean it, or is she just testing Benedick's love for her, or . . . any other reason that works for the production and the character they are rooted in. *Much Ado* is a play that can be fitted into many different cultures, geographical settings and periods. When I played Beatrice at the RSC in 2002, our production was firmly set in Sicily circa 1935, a society built on the notion of *omertà*, which emphasised family honour and kept males and females in very separate enclaves. This meant I could play 'Kill Claudio' as code for 'Kill your loyalty to your macho culture that knows and cares so little about who a woman is so long as she's a virgin. Grow up and grow a pair.'

The priest that was to marry Hero and Claudio comes up with a typical Shakespearean wheeze. He will put it out that Hero is dead. Her name will be cleared, and Claudio will be mortified and realise what an idiot he has been. Hero then poses as some relation (who coincidentally looks and sounds exactly like her) and when asked to take her as his bride, Claudio declares himself to be absolutely fine with that. Has he not learnt anything? What Hero feels about marrying such a dick is not stated. Nothing must stand in the way of the happy ending we are heading towards. There will be a double wedding, with Beatrice and Benedick marrying too; Don John will be punished and there will be much music and dancing.

It is a really delightful play with a witty couple at its heart. It was blissful to exchange flirtatious banter with the wonderfully funny and intelligent Nicholas Le Prevost. I had acted with him quite a lot previously, which helped with the familiarity Beatrice hints at in 'I know you of old'. It was also hilarious trying to get some of our very English cast to lower their centre of gravity and swap their Morris-dancers' bounce for a more salsa-esque swing of the hips at the wedding-party finale.

There has been some speculation about the title. On its

most simple surface it would seem to mean 'That was a lot of fuss about nothing. They all got in a stew about something that proved to be a lie.' But there is also a layer of meaning to the word 'nothing', which in Shakespeare's time was slang for a woman's sexual organs. She has no-thing between her legs. But also an unmarried woman who was not a virgin was a whore, worthless in the marriage market and therefore nothing, trash.

From Hero to Zero and Back

To me my name is Will-ful irony
For I am not the Hero of the play.
I just accept what others pile on me,
The cause of, not the agent in, the fray.

My poor relation Beatrice has more fun.
She's 'subplot' yet she gets to mock and move
With many an observation, quip and pun
While I stand by, the pretty po-faced juve,

The bride-to-be, the object of all eyes –
And object is the operative word –
Claudio considers me his prize,
A virtuous icon to be seen not heard.

I have a scene or two, I do admit,
Where I can show some bright prenuptial spark:
Alone with womenfolk I find my wit,
Queen of the boudoir, *there* I make my mark.

But with no mother to confide in me
'Tis Father's cronies I must move among.
They seldom see that other side of me
For something in their presence ties my tongue.

You see, I'm trying to grasp how slander vile,
An accusation paper thin and proofless,
Could turn a father's life-long love to bile,
Make him a stranger to me, cruel and ruthless.

A badly acted shadow pantomime
Was all it took to make him lose his faith.
A dumb show made him wish me dead, so I'm
Requiting him by staging my own death.

Now cousin Beatrice tests her Benedick:
'Of course she's innocent! You've all been conned!
You can't love both of us so take your pick.
Kill Claudio and break the macho bond.'

It never came to that, I'm glad to say.
However much I loathe the snivelling swine.
He's feeling guilty now and kneels to pray,
Exchanges pedestal for empty shrine.

He loves me now I'm dead, but quickly switches
When he espies my double (duh! It's me).
Again it is my image that bewitches –
Can this one work? I'll have to wait and see.

So this is how a misnamed girl called Hero
Learnt quickly how man's love can turn to doubt,
A faultless girl can fall so fast to zero –
A nothing that there's much ado about.

DESDEMONA

Othello

The play is about the mechanisms of jealousy, the manipulation of Othello by Iago, so in some sense it doesn't really matter who Desdemona is. She could be any woman. She is the object of a man's love and of his jealousy. We don't need to grow to know, like or admire her; we are on her side simply because she is a victim.

I have never played Desdemona, but I always wanted to know a bit more about her because there are indications in the story that she is adventurous, rule-breaking, passionate, open-minded, curious – marvellous qualities which become less important than her physical desirability as the plot unfolds.

As in other pieces in this book I am interested in the link between love and ownership. Treasuring something or somebody must always involve a commensurate fear of losing that thing or person, but ideally love between husband and wife should include friendship, mutual knowledge and trust. Othello does not seem to know Desdemona well enough to discredit Iago's insinuations that she is lusting after Cassio. If Othello had had more trust in Desdemona the person, Iago would not have been able to exploit his terror of losing his treasured possession.

Although I have never done the play, I have taken part in workshops and masterclasses playing Iago's wife Emilia in her brilliant exchange with Desdemona in Act IV, Scene 3. There are not many scenes in the canon in which two women are left alone to talk openly to one another, and to my mind these are some of Shakespeare's best. (Off the top of my head I can think of those between Olivia and Viola in *Twelfth Night*, Celia and Rosalind in *As You Like It* and even Mistresses Page and Ford in *The Merry Wives of Windsor*.)

In the privacy of Desdemona's chamber, the women can shelter from the male storm that is brewing outside and talk freely. Jealousy has turned Desdemona's husband into someone unfamiliar to her. Emilia's conversation hints at her own history with Iago, and the suggestion (admittedly from a paranoid Iago himself) that Othello may have had a relationship with her. Shakespeare makes none of this explicit, but it all provides a rich undertow to the scene and lends many interpretive choices to actors and directors. There is a humour and a candour in the scene, a real glimpse into the trust that can quickly form between two very different people just by dint of being women in a man's world.

At the top of the scene, Desdemona exposes the foreboding that has been plaguing her subconscious. At last she can share it:

> Good faith, how foolish are our minds!
> If I do die before thee prithee, shroud me
> In one of those same sheets.

Emilia's earthy wisdom sets Desdemona straight on the way men think, but the next thing to appear before Desdemona's newly opened eyes is her husband, lowering over her on the point of suffocating her.

I want to get behind Desdemona's eyes as she realises Othello is about to kill her. I want to be put back in touch with the love that existed between these two people before it was taken over by manipulators and intruders, judges and critics. I want to imagine those last seconds where Desdemona might try to pull Othello back to that original love. I want to look at that unthinkable moment when her lover becomes a stranger and then a murderer.

'Oh, these men, these men!'

Unique we were, Othello, you and I,
An 'us' we formed together to defy
All preconceptions, jealousies and fools.
I chose you, did the running, broke the rules.
Remember how we whispered by the sea,
Remember how we prized our secrecy?
How equally we felt that loving flood
That forced down dams and mingled in our blood.
Magnetic pulses folded into one,
You were my puma, I your spreading swan.
Would I dismantle that for Cassio?
Who got to you? That's what I want to know.
How easily the monster took its hold
In your sweet fertile soil and fearful soul.
Your wartime courage drained, you lost your head
And now believe the thing you most do dread.
I thought you knew me, lover, wife and friend.
Your treasured trust I never would misspend.
But poisoned words fed by a fellow man
Convince far more than woman's actions can.
Emilia hears my song and feeds my flame,
And teaches me that all men are the same.
I catch my breath, succumbing to your might.
I just woke up as you put out my light.

HERMIONE AND IMOGEN

The Winter's Tale and Cymbeline

Two quite different women but I want them to have a conversation about what they have in common: that is, husbands who very readily believe they are unfaithful and are prepared to kill them as a consequence. The men allow rumours and dubious evidence to eclipse everything they have learned from intimate private relationships with their wives (a common theme that I touch on with Hero and Desdemona).

Imogen is the daughter of Cymbeline, the king of an ancient Britain. Her husband, Posthumus, was raised alongside her in the court. Their childish love developed into a grown-up one and they have secretly married. He is banished very suddenly and so he leaves Britain for Italy, where he meets Iachimo (related by name as well as by his part in the plot to Iago). There follows a macho conversation about the comparative qualities of British versus Italian women, and in response to Posthumus's claims for his wife, Iachimo says, 'You must not so far prefer her 'fore ours of Italy,' and that he will prove Posthumus wrong in his faith in Imogen.

He travels to Britain, where he meets Imogen and later tricks his way into her chamber while she is asleep, and then returns to Posthumus with some admittedly pretty convincing 'proof' that he has enjoyed a night with her. He describes every detail of her room, the hangings on the walls; he produces a ring and a bracelet from her arm and describes a mole she has on her breast.

(So many people in fiction have moles on their breast there's a risk of devaluing this as proof of identity, but there you go . . .)

Outraged, Posthumus instructs his servant to kill Imogen and off goes the plot. There is a happy ending, but the play takes many a wondrous twist and turn to reach it.

For Hermione in *The Winter's Tale*, things get more serious before they resolve.

She is the daughter of a Russian emperor and married to Leontes, the King of Sicily, who is a jealous man. When he sees his pregnant wife 'paddling palms and pinching fingers . . . and making practised smiles' with his childhood friend Polixenes, King of Bohemia, it spins him into a frenzy of jealousy that leads to Hermione's imprisonment, the death of his young son and the banishment of his baby daughter Perdita. The Delphic Oracle, no less, proclaims Hermione's innocence and the valiant Paulina, a senior member of the household, punishes Leontes even further by pretending Hermione has died of grief. It's a wonder that she hasn't.

The first half of the play heads towards tragedy but the second half redeems everyone with some comedy and a happy ending. After sixteen years, during which Paulina has kept Hermione closeted away from the reclusive Leontes, the time has come for him to be brought before a statue of his wife. Paulina unveils this statue and the repentant Leontes is overcome by the likeness and touches her hand:

O, she's warm!

Well of course she is. She is his living, breathing wife. Everyone reckons that sixteen years is long enough for him to have suffered, but did Hermione have to suffer too? Would she really rediscover her love for Leontes after all that's happened? Speculations abound in my head.

Hermione and Imogen have theatrical sisters in Hero and in Desdemona, but each is isolated in her own play so they do not get to share their common plight.

I thought I would give at least two of these exasperated women the chance to have an off-loading session.

We Strumpets Must Stick Together

HERMIONE:

What's wrong with smiling eyes and paddling palms?
Polixenes is fun, I'll not pretend.
My husband seems to think he owns my charms,
Can't bear to share me with his childhood friend.

IMOGEN:

It seems to me he treats you as some treasure –
A thing to covet and to be displayed,
Not to be touched. But I say, 'Seize your pleasure!
Don't hide away. Don't let your beauty fade.'

HERMIONE:

And what of you? When Posthumus was jealous,
Based on unproven lies he'd merely heard,
Were you then tempted off the path? Do tell us.

IMOGEN:

The very thought of it is quite absurd!

HERMIONE (aside):

The lady does protest too much, I think.

IMOGEN (*after a pause*):

> I must confess I was a little smitten
> By Iachimo, and could have had a dalliance.
> You don't find flattery like that in Britain –
> It's true what people say about Italians.

HERMIONE:

> What stopped you then? Or did you follow through?

IMOGEN:

> I really can't think why I'm telling you . . .
> I turned him down, thank God, and saved my soul.
> But later to my bedchamber he crept
> And stole beneath my sheets and spied my mole;
> My better self pretended that I slept.

HERMIONE:

> Now that's the sort of romance that one misses.
> What else occurred? I beg you, paint the scene.

IMOGEN:

> Well, in my 'sleep' I did return his kisses.
> . . . You're very nosy for a noble queen.

HERMIONE:

> Forgive me. It's just better when we share
> The truth that stirs beneath our given text.

IMOGEN:

So my turn, then. Did you have an affair?
You feigned your death and so? What happened next?

HERMIONE:

Paulina, bless her, had a cunning plan.
She hid me first and then helped me escape.
For sixteen years I went from man to man
But all the time was haunted by a shape,
The growing shape of my beloved girl
Last seen a babe. My lost child Perdita
Was always sorely missing from my world
Until at last Paulina heard of her.

IMOGEN:

Cut to the chase. United in Act Five
Paulina now reveals the whole contrivance.
What happens now they know you are alive?

HERMIONE:

I took Leontes back . . . The rest is silence.

IMOGEN:

Oh well. Good luck and please let's talk some more –
It's been such fun. Now I must change my costume as
I'm dressed in boyish weeds and looking poor,
And might alarm my long-lost Posthumus.

But O, you men, you men! And your obsessions
That we will leave you when we love you dear.
By treating us as merely your possessions
You usher in the thing you most do fear.

OPHELIA

Hamlet

When I played Ophelia at the Royal Court in 1980, I was a young-looking, young-sounding thirty-year-old and professionally immature. As I said earlier, I was daunted by the company I had been thrown into after having only played with actors of roughly the same age and experience as myself. I had no idea how 'proper' plays were put on. I was used to doing any job on stage or backstage as well as loading sets onto a little van that took us to non-theatre venues all around the country.

Actors are taught to use whatever they are going through if it can be appropriately fed into the role they are playing, so this feeling of being in awe of everything and everyone around me could easily be transposed onto Ophelia's awe and intimidation by everything and everyone around *her*. She is pushed around, allowed very little autonomy and does not have a lot to say. I wasn't actually pushed around, but my own inner voice bullied me quite a lot, telling me that I didn't know what I was doing, that there was a way proper actors spoke Shakespeare and I wasn't doing it, etc. I didn't know how to rehearse and because we only had four weeks from first read-through to opening night, and because Ophelia doesn't have many scenes, I didn't spend a lot of time in the rehearsal room and had a lot of time to think and to build on my paranoia.

In my homework I made deep and complicated decisions about what was going on inside Ophelia's head, few of which could ever be demonstrated to the audience. It was an early lesson in playing small parts: you may totally inhabit your character and know all there is to know about them, but the play and the audience are not that concerned.

I also learned a lot about performance. Jonathan was electrically alive in every performance and this demanded a lot of spontaneity and accommodation from me. The 'get thee to a nunnery' scene was different every night and I couldn't wait to get at it again the next day and see what would *happen*. Ideally, theatre performance is something that *happens* each night, rather than something planned and exactly repeated.

I always kept a core of Ophelia to myself. Neither the cast, the director nor the audience would know all my secrets. If Ophelia herself had had such a core, rather than the fragile ego she has in the play, she might have been able to rebel against her restrictions: the rules of the Danish court, the overbearing control of her father, her brother (who sets himself up as a kind of deputy mini-father) and her forbidden sexual lust and longing for Hamlet.

Madness is a good way out. Madness releases Ophelia into lawlessness, and vulgarity. It also released me from my initially inhibited performance to something more my own, a kind of 'You can't tell me what I'm thinking!' to the theatre establishment and the critics (a mostly imagined convocation of men in suits and grandes dames in pearls, who judged me for many years to come). Plugging back into Ophelia for this book I can dream of a different outcome to her story. And why shouldn't it be true? It's only a play after all.

Ophelia Fooled Ya

'Twas overhearing Hamlet that inspired me –
Six syllables to weigh the price of life.
T'obey or not t'obey had been *my* question,
But fatherless henceforth I could take flight.
To die, perchance cheat death, and leave my body
To hibernate awhile then reappear
A reinvented unconnected person,
Not sicklied o'er with thinking or with fear.
Observing Hamlet carefully, I aped him;
Like him escaped by faking antic ways.
If he was mad north-west I'd be his tailwind,
Distract them with distraction, seeming crazed.
From there it was a breeze to stage my drowning.
I sought the help of one who digs the graves.
'Beside Poor Yorick's corpse there is an orphan
Not buried yet. I'll see how much she weighs.'
Then later as an unobserved observer,
I watched them trail my understudy's bier.
It worked a treat. So totally enshrouded
She fooled them, and they drenched her with their
      tears.
Did Hamlet or my brother howl the loudest?
(I own I had to eavesdrop on their griefs.)
The sad truth is whichever way you sound it,
The person they were mourning wasn't me.

One last obedient act I did for Hamlet:
He bade me to a nunnery, so I went.

And oh, what marvellous people I have found here,
Encloistered in these deep sequestered walls.
No saintly nuns to speak of but some sisters
That narrow tongues do fast, loose women call;
The learned and the simple, young and ancient,
The harlots and the headstrong, wits and bores,
The accidental mothers and their offspring,
Creative, crafty, cracked or merely flawed.
Their heads held high, their feet upon the ground.
I fit right in among the lost and found.

CRESSIDA

Troilus and Cressida

I have never played Cressida, though I have studied her speeches for various masterclasses given by the late, great John Barton. Barton was a kind of Shakespeare guru who unlocked the language of his plays for so many actors in the UK, the USA and other English-speaking cultures round the world. By unlocking the language I mean that he showed us how the clues to playing the parts lay within the text itself, within its rhythms, structures, particular choice of imagery. That is where a character is found and nowhere else. That is the particular nature of what we call 'language plays'. No amount of add-on characteristics, funny voices or wayward interpretations will work if you go against the flow of the language and ignore Shakespeare's own guidelines hidden within it. Barton taught us to find and read those guidelines rather like a crossword-puzzler learns the hallmarks of a certain setter.

Troilus and Cressida was Barton's favourite play because of its ingenious combination of political and philosophical arguments, thrashed out in war rooms and army camps, alongside an intense young love affair conducted in private chambers. I find it a very puzzling play full of brilliant speeches, full of Shakespeare's anger, but my interest occasionally drifts away when we get too deeply into the army camp scenes with lazy Achilles and petulant Patroclus. Ho hum. Sorry.

It is one thing to study a text but it's another thing entirely to imbibe it and then be able to pour it out to an audience as if the words came from inside your own head. For this reason I don't feel very qualified to write about Cressida, not having undergone that journey of learning her words, playing the part and interacting with others in a production.

Despite this, I needed to write a piece about her because there is an inconsistency in her depiction that poses a problem not just for the actor playing her but for the women in the audience. Shakespeare has her open her heart to us in the first half of the play and we root for her in her love of Troilus. We are grateful for some wit and light relief from the backdrop of war, and Shakespeare seems to be very much on her side. Then the centre of the play shifts and Shakespeare seems to abandon her to hostile male judgement.

Cressida is swapped in a kind of prisoner exchange at the request of her father, who has gone over to the Greek side and asked that his daughter be brought to him while an important Trojan prisoner is released. Cressida only learns of this on waking from her first night of love with Troilus. With no time to think and no possibility of argument, she is whisked away to the Greek camp and thereafter we hear very little from her.

She is observed from across a field, as it were, through the gaze of Troilus, whose interpretation of her actions we are supposed to go along with. She has betrayed him with another man and that is all we need to know. It is as though Shakespeare suddenly goes off her, and those of us who have enjoyed and admired her are left stranded and confused.

There are many possible reasons for Cressida's behaviour or betrayal even, but Shakespeare doesn't throw any light on them; nor does he give Cressida a speech that justifies her actions. A character who has shared so much with us suddenly turns her shoulder and leaves us guessing.

The theme of war takes over and Shakespeare's own cynicism

seems to predominate. The play was probably written around 1602 and *Hamlet* was written around 1601. Just prior to that time Shakespeare wrote some of his more sympathetic women – Rosalind, Viola, Olivia, Beatrice, Lady Percy – but after 1600, things change. Various writers have suggested that something happened in Shakespeare's own love life that embittered him to women and love in general. We can't forget that a writer has a life going on in parallel to their work, which interweaves with and influences the latter. Maybe he was indeed going through a time when he didn't trust women and the result is that Gertrude in *Hamlet* and Cressida here suffer as a result. If this is so, happily it was just a phase, as later on he wrote plenty of great women.

The Trojan War, which is the setting for *Troilus and Cressida*, was kicked off by the abduction of Greek Helen by Trojan Paris. Helen is the bartered war bride *par excellence*. Cressida too is played, traded and tossed from one male to another, and fends for herself pretty admirably.

The two women have much in common but the play doesn't give them any chance to connect.

Cressida is silent about her motives in flirting with the Greek generals and giving herself (we suppose) to Diomedes. Her scene with him consists of whispers in his ear and half-sentences which, as interpreted by Troilus looking on from a distance with pained and jealous eyes, amounts to simple betrayal.

After that scene, all we hear from her is:

Ah, poor our sex! This fault in us I find,
The error of our eye directs our mind:

Hmm. I wonder. Is this Shakespeare speaking or Cressida?

If I had played the part, I would have had to find a way through her moral maze, but not having inhabited her in that way I am left with speculations and can get no nearer to

Shakespeare's truth. I decided to focus on the Cressida we get to know in the early part of the play: the self-knowing philosopher, the questioner. The way she seems to understand so much about the restrictions on a woman's life, she feels quite radical and modern. I tried to imagine her as the writer of a column in some timeless women's magazine in which she comments on a few themes, leaving us to make the connections.

Cressida Reflects on War, Virginity and Pandering to Men

I

On Pandarus

I call him Uncle Scandalous for fun,
Provoke him, prod him, parry, dodge his darts,
Delight in innuendo, love a pun,
But playful banter hides a fragile heart.

Quick-witted, headstrong, old before my years:
That's how he sees me, thinks that I can take it.
I'll never lift my mask to show my fears.
If I don't *feel* courageous I can fake it.

I do not trust his advocating Troilus
To be my mate. There's something he won't tell us.
He sees young love and maybe would despoil us.
I don't know why but I suspect he's jealous.

Fatigue has killed his kindness, marred his mind.
Long years of war make cynics of us all
So I'll continue to give back in kind
While round my true heart I will build a wall.

II

War Whores: 1. Helen

What's Helen's fault that it should start a war,
A war so old the cause is long forgot?
'Twas Paris stole her, *he* who broke the law,
Yet armies cursed her beauty as the fault.
The common soldier couldn't give a fart –
What's he to Helena or she to him,
That he should perish for some foreign tart,
Be robbed of youth upon a cuckold's whim?
And who could Helen turn to for support?
To mad Cassandra or Queen Hecuba?
Like me, she floundered motherless at court,
Learned to outglare the leering lecherer,
Fought with her looks, re-shaped her supple mind
To be accepted in the Trojan fold.
If only we two 'whores' had dared combine,
How differently the story might be told.

War Whores: 2. Cressida

I too was bartered, brutally uprooted
From native Troy and from my lover's arms
(I note the double meaning of that word;
That can embrace or have a soldier suited).
Stripped of all status, circled by Greek men,
I flirted with the foe to fend them off.
With Diomed's protection for a while
I played for time and hoped I might survive
To outlive war, return to Troilus's side.
But oh! My 'loose' behaviour in the camp

(Prompted by what? A need for company?
A sense that any way I turned I'd lose?)
Left me a rootless vagabond of war,
My body open to their trespassing.
Though 'tis *my* 'trespass' that outlives my time.
The anti-heroine of epic plays
Stuck with my own words sticking in my craw,
My name synonymous with fickleness.
The archetype of female treachery.
'False Cressid' ever trapped in timeless lines
Created by a venerated Bard.

III

On Virginity

What's in a word? What is 'virginity'?
Why is our value so tied up therein?
Is't men that prize this untouched quality?
I think it is. To me it is no sin
To give it free and then no more possess it.
There is no alteration in my soul,
No change intrinsical. I am still Cressid,
I cannot 'lose' what leaves me feeling whole.

If women made the rules what would we fear
About a little split in Hymen's tissue –
A membrane curtain with a tear,
A channel for a new creation's issue?
Would snooping women stoop to scrutinise
A spit of blood upon a nuptial sheet
To test the value of a husband's prize?
I doubt it, ladies. Let's have done with it!

My tongue is reckless. I must chasten it
Till Our Time comes. Oh let us hasten it!

IV

On Virtue

Look in your own glass, ladies, and reflect,
Our 'virtue' lies in passive maidenhood
Most prized and trusted if we stay intact
Not *active* virtue as in *doing* good.
So men miss out for they will never know us,
Since love and ownership are interwoven.
As foreign states they seek to overthrow us
Before our true integrity is proven

Now look therein again and now erase
Your men's appraisals and th'effects thereof
All shame reflected in your Master's gaze
Dictating fates you are not mistress of.
Hold up your head and listen to your heart –
Your judgement's best when they are both in play –
'Tis when you own your virtue that life starts.
Cherish your appetites and seize the day.

V

On Time

From ancient seabed I come up for air,
Swimming from my century to yours,
Find water drops have merely brushed the stones.
Still women weep while men still go to wars
Unwinnable, pick cities to the bone,
Their displaced people, sick and in despair,
Turned back from borders like a beating tide
That has no choice but stronger to return.
And in this havoc hearts grow thick with hate,
Turned inward or displayed in proud parades
Too often misdirected 'gainst the slaves
And not the unseen hand that holds the chain.
Though you have told yourselves that much has changed,
The topsoil shifts. The twisted roots remain.

OCTAVIA

Antony and Cleopatra

I often forget that Octavia, not Ophelia, was my first professional Shakespearean role, because she is so easily forgettable. She has barely two scenes and speaks a mere thirty-six lines. She is depicted as a bloodless pawn, married off to the newly widowed Mark Antony to seal a political alliance between him and her brother Octavius Caesar (later the emperor Augustus). Antony has been absent without leave in Cleopatra's bed in Egypt and Octavius needs to win him back to his Roman duties. I played the part at the Duke's Playhouse in Lancaster aged twenty-three. Those were the much-missed days of repertory theatre, to which a young actor could move on after drama school and continue their apprenticeship playing everything from Shakespeare to pantomime, with a new production to learn every three or four weeks. I have one record of that production: a black-and-white photo of me standing between two beefy-chested male actors who look at one another over my head while I tilt imploring eyes into my brother's face. Each man holds me by a hand and my skinny arms hang like limp ropes between them. It is an eloquent image of a character who can say of herself 'The Jove of power make me most weak, most weak, your reconciler.'

Years later, I played Cleopatra. I knew that the scene in which she learns that Antony has married Octavia is noted for its comedy but for Cleopatra herself it is extremely painful. The audience laughs hysterically at her melodramatic reaction and at her horrendous treatment of the slave who brings her the news. They don't take her distress seriously because they have seen how pathetic her rival really is. Also, in a scene just before this they have heard Antony say,

> I will to Egypt:
> And though I make this marriage for my peace,
> I' the east my pleasure lies.

In other words, we know already that he is about to return to her irresistible arms, and we are pleased about it.

In Shakespeare's play the marriage is over almost before it begins. The historical truth about Octavia is that she and Antony spent enough time together to produce two daughters, and although it was a political marriage and he did spend a lot of time travelling back and forth to Egypt, eventually abandoning Octavia and marrying Cleopatra, they were not a bad team. Octavia often acted as mediator between her husband and her brother when they came close to dangerous disagreements. She accompanied Antony on his provincial rounds and was quite a vital hands-on supporter in some of his military campaigns.

She settled with him in Athens and presided over a household which included the offspring of Antony's former marriages, those of her own earlier marriage, and the two daughters they had together. Later on, when Antony and Cleopatra had both died by suicide, Octavia took over the guardianship of their children – all this as well as fulfilling various public duties: opening libraries, welcoming Roman armies back from victories abroad and being an effective negotiator and diplomat on her brother's behalf.

It suited Shakespeare's plot to depict Octavia as nice but dull, so that the audience will root for the wayward couple of the play's title. They may passingly pity Octavia but in truth they want her out of the way so they can get on with the main action.

Centuries earlier, Seneca had also taken an attitude to Octavia, depicting her as having entirely retreated from the world in mourning for her young son Marcellus, but that doesn't chime with what I learnt about the real woman so I thought I would let her set the record straight. Of course, the *real* Octavia would consider this yet another appropriation of her story. Who can ever know the full truth?

Numquam Verum Corrumpere Bonam Fabulam

or *Never Let the Truth Get in the Way of a Good Story**

First Seneca the Poet chose to wrap me
In mourning for my son, in dusty grief.
In shuttered villas thought he could entrap me
Forever blotting out the glare of life.

Then Shakespeare needed me to justify
Mark Antony's pathetic misbehaviour
Pursuing his Egyptian butterfly,
So I became the tawdry moth Octavia.

In fact I was not 'dull of tongue' nor 'dwarfish'
As Cleopatra wanted to believe.
Rewriting what her cowering slave reported.
Her self-deception earned him a reprieve.

I did emerge from Seneca's bereavement,
Resumed my public offices in Rome
And, this perhaps my most unsung achievement,
Raised Cleopatra's orphans as my own.

The whelps she bred with Antony in Egypt
I welcomed to the bosom of my brood;
I cannot claim affection was immediate,
But duty led the way and love ensued.

---

* I confess this is not some ancient Latin aphorism. I just put a rather good phrase I had heard into Google Translate and this is what it came up with.

In History as in Art the 'facts' are pliable.
Dramatic 'truth' is fun but unreliable.
The truth I lived is drained of all its glory.
Thus poets use my life to suit their story.

PRINCESS KATHERINE OF FRANCE

Henry V

In Act III, scene 4 of the history play *Henry V*, the French Princess Katherine is being given an English lesson by her lady-in-waiting Alice. It is a welcome comic scene in a male-driven play about war. Alice is not the greatest expert on English, so Shakespeare has fun with some dodgy double-entendres. In their mispronunciations she calls the gown a 'coun', or 'con', which means vagina; the foot is misheard as 'foutre', which means to have sex, and the elbow becomes the 'bilbow' – not too far off 'dildo'. I checked the last and it was first recorded at the end of the sixteenth century

I have tried to slip in some slightly blue but innocent mispronunciations and misuses but mostly I have had fun with some well-known French sayings.

The historical Katherine was the daughter of Charles VI of France and Isabeau of Bavaria. Her marriage to Henry V was one of convenience, uniting two countries that had been at war for hundreds of years.

Despite the political expedience of the marriage, it seems to have been a loving one and the attraction between the two of them was pretty immediate.

Although it didn't last long (Henry died two years after they married) I want to celebrate this good match.

A liaison amoureuse

Le Rozbiff King of Angleterre –
The one with poudding-basin 'air –
All coq because he won la guerre
'As asked me for my 'and.

I said to please 'im was my gueule
And for a fille, I'll suit him well.
He says, 'Tu est spirituelle,'
And told me I was 'cul'.

Our Franglais somewhat lacks nuance,
Mais en tout cas one gets the sense
And honi soit qui mal y pense.
We could just laisser faire,

Ça n'importe pas we've barely met,
C'est bon, our Royal tête à tête.
It's almost accompli, le fait –
I feel it's déjà vu.

If he could let 'is heir to grow
He'd make a very 'andsome beau.
I've never really 'ad one, so . . .
I'll give the Royal 'Oui'.

MARIANA
AND DIANA

Measure for Measure and
All's Well That Ends Well

First, a word about the bed trick. The bed trick is a plot device drawn from traditional literature and folklore. In its standard and most common form, a man believes he is going to a sexual assignation with a certain woman but, not being able to see in the dark, he doesn't realise that another woman has taken the original woman's place.

Shakespeare is said to have got the idea from *The Decameron* by Boccaccio (who no doubt pinched it from someone else) and he uses the bed trick in his two dark comedies, *All's Well That Ends Well* and *Measure for Measure*.

In *All's Well*, the (non-)hero Bertram thinks he is going to have sex with Diana, a woman he is trying to seduce; Helena, the protagonist, who loves him (for some reason we can't quite understand), takes Diana's place in the darkened bedchamber, and so consummates a marriage she was promised by the King of France but that Bertram has run away from.

In *Measure for Measure*, Angelo expects to have sex with Isabella, the heroine, but Mariana, the woman Angelo had been engaged to marry but abandoned, slips into his bed in Isabella's place.

It's win-win for the women and lose-lose for the dastardly men.

I want this to be a celebration, albeit with a slightly bitter edge. Perhaps it could even be a song, if someone would like to set it to music.

Duet of the Interchangeables

DIANA:

We want to put a word in for our Will,
Remind you that he's often on our side:
The plays that we are in should fit the bill
To show it's often men he can't abide.

Abuse of power is topmost on his list
Of hateful things he labours to expose.
Hypocrisy, wherever it exists,
A deadly sin that gets right up his nose.

MARIANA:

Giovanni Boccaccio coined the idea
And William borrowed it – nothing wrong there.
We've both played the bed trick, for so it is named,
In separate plays and we don't feel ashamed.
We rather rejoice in our cunning and craft –
We came out on top and the audience laughed.

DIANA:

I hated Count Bertram's unwanted advances
And then I met Helena! What were the chances?
On learning that Bert wanted me in his bed
She offered me money to go in my stead.
'There's no need to pay me, I couldn't give tuppence,
As long as you promise he'll get his comeuppance.'

I knew that for Helena All was *not* Well.
She loved him, I didn't, and he couldn't tell
The difference between us. In pitch black it seems
He bedded and boarded the girl of his dreams,
Enjoyed her all right, with a ring it was sealed
And Helen was pregnant when all was revealed.
I'm proud of my part in breaking the deadlock
But how Well is an End if you're *duped* into wedlock?

DIANA AND MARIANA (*chorus*):

Oh women be wary, the lesson is stark:
We all look the same to a man in the dark.

MARIANA:

My story is different 'cause Angelo loathed
The thought of our marriage, though *we* were betrothed.
He'd gladly engaged in premarital sex
Till my fortune went missing in one of those wrecks
So useful to playwrights. Now Isabel comes,
She's being blackmailed for sex – that's a no-no for nuns.
If she doesn't bed Angelo her brother dies.
Seems the 'crime' of adultery only applies
To whom Angelo says it does by his decree.
Misnamed and misogynist, no Angel he!
The bed trick should sort it so everyone wins
'Cept Angelo! I'll make him pay for his sins!

DIANA AND MARIANA (*chorus*):

You men now be wary, the lesson is stark:
We all look the same to a man in the dark.

DARK LADY
SONNET I

(with some reference
to Shakespeare's
Sonnets 18, 130 and 144)

I shan't get into the speculation as to who the Dark Lady was. There has been endless discussion about it, and I am sorry, but unless some treasure trove of her or Shakespeare's diaries is discovered I don't think we will ever know. I like her remaining a mystery. I like Shakespeare weaving strands around her, designed to keep her hidden. I just loved the idea of trying to write something in strict sonnet form. No hubris involved. No attempt to match the Bard. I think this speaks for itself, but the idea came to me that the Muse may feel more mortal than the verse.

His Dark Lady Answers Back

He called me dun, dark, dwarfish, wiry-haired
Ethiop, temptress, not so fair as black.
Loathing his love, no fault of mine is spared,
And being no Bard I cannot answer back.
Shall *my* eternal summer never fade?
Or did he mean his pretty fair-skinned lord,
The goodie-goodie angel, not this jade –
His baddie mistress and his reek-breathed bawd?
I'll never know, and nor will countless scholars,
However long they pore o'er dusty books,
And knowing they can't know gives me some solace;
I'll fear no more to lose my dusky looks.
So long as men can breathe or eyes can see
So long there's just a chance it could be me.

LADY ANNE

Richard III

I have never played Lady Anne myself but, sitting in the audience watching *Richard III*, I have wanted to understand the woman better. The terrifying momentum of the play comes from Richard's ambition and neither he nor the play can afford to stop long enough to investigate what makes Lady Anne switch, in one scene, from loathing the man who murdered her husband and her father-in-law to – breathtakingly – agreeing to be his wife!

Admittedly it takes some time. The scene is long with many a change of tactic on Richard's side. Anne gives him a run for his money and bats back everything he throws at her. This is a great example of two characters picking up on one another's sentences and returning them with a twist. This kind of attentiveness indicates many helpful things to an actor playing these parts: the scrutiny of a predator, the watchfulness of the prey, something shared – love or fear, a sexual chemistry which can be attraction or revulsion, or a mixture of both. Richard realises what an amazing feat he has achieved:

> Was ever woman in this humour woo'd?
> Was ever woman in this humour won? . . .
> What! I, that kill'd her husband and his father . . .
> And yet to win her . . .

We in the audience are astonished too. How did that happen?

Here chemistry really counts in the casting: two brilliant actors without the chemistry will leave the audience perplexed and unmoved. But if the actors in question can create a believable physical charge between the two characters, then this seemingly nonsensical scene takes on a hypnotising logic.

For all the negatives Richard himself describes about his physical appearance, he must be charismatic in some deep, dark way, and there must be something in Anne's make-up that needs what he is offering. She is vulnerable and directionless in the throes of grief. The man she most fears and hates has some deadly pull on her.

In this piece I see Anne as bewildered by her own behaviour, trying to justify it with that self-deluding rationale, 'Maybe I can change him . . .'

Whatever rationale Anne finds within herself doesn't last long and neither does her life. She is soon to be poisoned by Richard to make way for a more advantageous marriage to Elizabeth of York, and Richard's triumph is itself short-lived. It's important to remember that this is Shakespeare's version of the story. It all makes great drama and is a brilliant examination of megalomania, but the historical accuracy is still very open to debate.

What we do know is that the long Wars of the Roses between the House of York (white rose) and the House of Lancaster (red rose) came to an end when Richard was killed at the Battle of Bosworth Field in 1485. Shakespeare has him famously crying out 'A horse! a horse! my kingdom for a horse!' and thanks to that horse not showing up the Tudor dynasty began. Anne was well out of it.

Was Ever Woman in This Humour Won?

What was I thinking? Oh, how frail a mind!
To let a monster thus to mould my moans
And bend my proud hostility to his will.

How did it happen? Was it loss of fear?

Fear lent my tongue a whip to lash at him,
To parry every thrust and stab of his,
Exchange my spitted hate for his false love,
Turn twisted words back to his twisted limbs.
A long, protracted interchange we had –
Not many women could have so endured –
But then my planted feet begin to give.
His spidery shanks had formed a viscous web
Of honey'd words that wound me in their trap.
O, feeble dame to feed on flattery,
Still knowing that the words were breathed from hell.
Can I blame grief that held me in a haze?
A madness that had cut me loose from reason?
Or was another alien force at work,
A kind of magnet to a morbid soul,
A strange attraction to my mirror'd self?
I feared him less and even pitied him,
This evil poet, runt Plantagenet.
The Boar of England did not need my hate
To heap upon his own well-honed self-loathing.
No. Rather might my acquiescence work
To purge the festering swill of vengeful thoughts
That his unwished-for celibacy brewed.

Oh wrong and wrong and wrong on all counts wrong!
King Richard now discards me as his queen
In favour of a bloodline better bred.

The throne of England proves too strong a lure,
The path to it is littered with the dead,
Both red and white. A plague on both their houses.
I leave the stage with pity for them all.

PORTIA

Julius Caesar

I n *Julius Caesar*, Portia has two scenes: a fairly substantial one with her husband and another brief one with a servant. For the main scene with Brutus, Shakespeare seems to have taken the story pretty much straight from historical accounts by Plutarch and others. Brutus is planning to assassinate his erstwhile friend Caesar, who has become increasingly despotic and is about to crown himself king. This would mean the start of a dynasty of inherited power that goes against everything the Roman Republic was built on, namely a democratic rule of the people (male people) as represented by the Senate (male Senators).

The real Portia was quite politically engaged. Her father, Cato, was a sworn enemy of Julius Caesar and his faction stood for the rule of the people against what was seen as Caesar's growing autocracy. He opposed Caesar in the Great Roman Civil War and, like all good Romans, he committed suicide when he was defeated in battle. Suicide was an honour and indeed a duty in defeat. Brutus did the same, and although it is not certain how Portia died, Shakespeare built on the idea that she too killed herself, in her case out of grief at Brutus's expected defeat at Philippi.

Portia hated Caesar for her father's sake and would have been in favour of his assassination. But Brutus kept the plot a secret from her until she gouged a slice from her thigh. Her physical courage so impressed Brutus that he gave in and divulged the plan. Again, Shakespeare's version is taken directly from historical accounts.

The scene at the start of Act II is closely related to the scene between Hotspur and his wife Kate, Lady Percy, in Act II of *Henry IV part I*. An intuitive wife catches her husband sleeplessly wandering in the middle of the night and demands to know his business. Both men give their wives a sort of 'don't bother your pretty head about it', but whereas Hotspur keeps up the obfuscation (in the most charming way), Brutus respects his wife as the daughter of a politician and opponent of Caesar, and agrees to share his dilemma. From the whole atmosphere of the scene and Portia's knowing way with Brutus, we infer a fairly equal marriage, and so I want to hear more from this woman who understood so much about politics but was excluded by law and tradition.

What if *she* had got up in the marketplace to address the crowd after Caesar's death? Might she not be more persuasive than Brutus, who makes a good lawyer-like defence of the assassination but lacks the common touch? She would make the same argument that Caesar's overreaching ambition was bound to lead to a dictatorship if it hadn't already, and that the assassins had acted on behalf of the people and to preserve the ideals of the Roman Republic.

Might not her sincerity go to the hearts of the crowd more deeply and lastingly than Mark Antony's showy oratory? There is no denying Antony's brilliance as he puts an ironic spin on Brutus's reputation as 'an honourable man', but Portia might unite where Antony deliberately divides with the intent to rule. Maybe having a woman in the mix would broaden the people's choice between one man who is somewhat dull and awkward and another who is a manipulative fake. (Ring any bells?)

I am no political orator, so I had the same struggle to express myself as I supposed the unpractised public speaker Portia might have had.

The italicised lines are from Shakespeare's original.

Portia Holds Up the Mirror

Oh Romans! Patience! Please hear Portia speak!
I grant I am a woman; but withal
A woman that Lord Brutus took to wife:
I grant I am a woman; but withal
A woman well-reputed, Cato's daughter.
But I am more than this one's wife or that one's child,
I am a woman with a tongue to speak,
A heart to hear and vision to impart.
My heritage taught me to understand
What lay behind the posturing of men.
Their discourse was my childhood alphabet,
Rome's politics my nursery and my school.
I grant I have scant knowledge of your lives
But I know this: that Caesar kept you tame
By filling up your bellies just enough
To keep your minds away from his true goals,
And bend your eyes away from shameful sights.
He killed ambition in you, doused your pride,
And now like cringing beasts you howl and whine,
As if by dying he abandoned you.
Think for yourselves and question *why* these men
Would kill this Caesar whom they once did love.
This Caesar aimed to be a lifelong king
And have his heirs inherit all his power.
Is that the aim of a republic? No!
We Romans don't believe in privilege
Inherited through consanguinity.
Dynastic roots are known for their tenacity,
Embedded family ties are hard to fight.

'Twas this my husband laboured to prevent –
For Brutus *is* an honourable man,
Who loves his country more than any king.
Prefers the demos to a deity.
All this his clumsy, clichéd words belie,
So you prefer the sugar-coated tongue,
The vanity of Antony's allure
(For 'ego' is a very Roman word).
His rhetoric is mere hypocrisy,
He twists the knife of language in your hearts
While railing 'gainst 'Great' Caesar's dagger-wounds.
For my part I do fear that shedding blood
Can only bring on brutish retribution,
A cycle of perpetual blinkered blame.
Democracy needs vision to survive,
It needs us all to cultivate our minds,
To challenge lies and think of better ways.
But you want only this day's bread and wine,
And care not for the future of your kind.
Oh that I were a man! I could prevent
Th'unleashing of a pointless civil war.
I can't o'erleap this sorrow to a time
When women may command a wiser world
So now I dream of self-delivered death
As reason turns to poison in my head.
My husband cannot hear of my despair;
My thoughts fly out, my words die on the air.

(*At the end we see this is all spoken in her chamber to her looking-glass.*)

ISABELLA

Measure for Measure

M easure for Measure is loosely categorised as a comedy but is often called a 'problem play'. It deals with very dark subjects: sexual abuse, abuse of power, the lawlessness of some lawmakers, adultery, venereal disease to name but a few. There are comic characters and some comedy scenes, but it is a black humour that laughs in the face of decadence and death.

The play is set in Vienna, where the ruling duke has abdicated temporarily and set up Angelo as his deputy governor. Angelo is out to clean up the streets and the brothels, and wants to make an example of a young Claudio, who has got his girlfriend pregnant out of wedlock. He sentences him to death.

Enter Claudio's sister Isabella, a novice nun, to fight for her brother's life and try to persuade Angelo to show some mercy.

Isabella has a wonderful moral integrity which she pits against the hypocrisy of the society that rules her. We love her speaking truth to power (although she loses many of us in her fanatical religiosity). When she is given the choice between sleeping with the odious Angelo or leaving her innocent brother to die, she says 'more than our brother is our chastity' and goes off to prepare Claudio for death. He seems to go along with the idea for her sake but then has a turnabout, with what I think is one of the most brilliant speeches ever written about death:

Ay, but to die, and go we know not where;
To lie in cold obstruction and to rot;
This sensible warm motion to become
A kneaded clod; and the delighted spirit
To bathe in fiery floods, or to reside
In thrilling region of thick-ribbed ice;
To be imprison'd in the viewless winds,
And blown with restless violence round about
The pendent world; or to be worse than worst
Of those that lawless and incertain thought
Imagine howling: 'tis too horrible!
The weariest and most loathed worldly life
That age, ache, penury and imprisonment
Can lay on nature is a paradise
To what we fear of death.

Isabella, being convinced of a heavenly afterlife if one behaves well in this one, is unsympathetic.

It is a hard part to play, and although I was offered the role a couple of times, for reasons of bad timing I never was able to.

What I did do, however, was to play out the two main Isabella/Angelo scenes in a couple of masterclasses given by John Barton and Adrian Noble.

In those workshops, my minimal experience of Isabella taught me a lasting lesson; you could call it 'The Argument's the Thing'. So much of how a Shakespeare speech (and therefore character) works is through argument. Even a soliloquy is an argument of sorts. When someone stands on stage alone and delivers a soliloquy it can be seen as a sort of pull-in on a highway where you can turn off the road and have a breather. But a play can't come to a halt. A soliloquy is not a static rumination. It is a development of the action.

A character posits a problem – an immediate reaction to

something that has happened. Then they wrestle with that problem and argue with themselves until they come to some kind of resolution which tilts the play forward into the next action. Holding on to the argument is a safeguard against a generalised wash of emotion. Even in grief a character in Shakespeare pits one thought against the next until they can emerge from the confusion of feelings and carry on. Argument is muscular and skeletal. Poetry is not high-flown language for its own sake but a precise selection of words and imagery that serve an argument. No word in Shakespeare is wasted or unspecific.

The way that Angelo and Isabella relate to one another is through argument. Doing these scenes taught me what one should do as an actor anyway, namely to listen. These antagonists have to listen with every fibre of their being; it is a question of survival, of winning the game. Much like the scene between Lady Anne and Richard III, Isabella and Angelo pick up one another's words and throw them back with an attentiveness that produces a sort of chemistry – a possible sexual chemistry. Shakespeare uses it in love scenes (famously in *Romeo and Juliet*, when the two first meet and play with words to form a perfect sonnet), or in conspiratorial scenes, as in *Macbeth*, between Macbeth and Lady Macbeth just after Macbeth has murdered Duncan. The pulse of the scene races. They seem to infect one another with fear.

LADY MACBETH:

Did not you speak?

MACBETH:

When?

LADY MACBETH:

　Now.

MACBETH:

　As I descended?

LADY MACBETH:

　Ay.

There is also a beautiful exchange between Olivia and Viola in *Twelfth Night*, where they play a semi-dangerous tit for tat:

OLIVIA:

　I prithee, tell me what thou thinkest of me.

VIOLA:

　That you do think you are not what you are.

OLIVIA:

　If I think so, I think the same of you.

VIOLA:

　Then think you right: I am not what I am.

There are countless examples of this requirement to observe one another's rhythms and images: it is like an instruction from Shakespeare to the actor.

The audience can sense when this is working well, and the scenes between Angelo and Isabella can become nail-bitingly charged. We love Isabella's fearless clarity. We are mesmerised and sickened by Angelo's intransigence and then horrified to learn where his close scrutiny of Isabella has been leading: to the male fantasy of seducing a nun away from her devotion to chastity.

In the wake of the Harvey Weinstein, Jeffrey Epstein and Jimmy Savile cases, Isabella's cry to the audience once Angelo has left –

> To whom should I complain? Did I tell this,
> Who would believe me?

– has obvious echoes for modern-day audiences and we want to shout back 'We do! We believe you! Things have changed!' The actor might hear us, but we could never reach the character.

The actor exists in the same time and space as the audience and is aware of them, but the character they are playing is trapped in a different time and space. The audience is moved by the character's plight but cannot intervene to help them.

I was a bit over-ambitious to think I could encapsulate the central paradox of live performance, but I hope the reader will come with me some of the way at least.

Isabella Reaches Out

To whom should I complain? I look to you –
Spectators seated in another time,
You distant witnesses of present harm.
Who will believe my story, in *my* world,
In vile Vienna where we lay our scene,
Where diabolic Angelo holds sway,
Personifying Law and Governance?
He relishes his brief terrestrial power
And would condemn me to eternal fire
To lose the love of Him that I adore
In order that my brother shall not die.
What would you do, I ask you, in my place?
'A little act,' you say, 'to save a life.'
Ay, but to die of shame and loss of self,
To be invaded, tainted and defiled,
Defined forever by a violent act,
Perhaps to birth a babe who shares his blood,
Imprisoned in a body false as sin,
Wrapped in revulsion at my creeping skin,
It is too horrible to think of.
My words evince your pity and your rage,
But none of you can change the drama's course.
Between us, the imaginary wall –
That mutual pact, that veil of make-believe –
Conspires to mock our common impotence.
For centuries we've gathered in the gloom,
In tiers and rows all breathing the same air,
Hoping our earthly boundaries to transcend.
So many Isabellas have reached out

Across that chasm blindly in the dark,
Believing that her God will answer her.
So many women quite outside the play
Are either cowed and silenced by self-blame,
Or if they dare, stand shouting to the wind
O'er silent canyons deaf with disbelief.

LADY MACBETH

Macbeth

Lady Macbeth is a small speaking part, but she punches well above her weight. There are characters in world literature that are so well known to us we almost believe they once existed. A perfect example is Sherlock Holmes, whose home at 221B Baker Street is constantly packed with his fans. This is especially true of many of Shakespeare's characters, who achieve such global familiarity and immortality that they become the archetype for a type of personality. Hamlet, the indecisive overthinker, is one such and Lady Macbeth, the dangerous female power behind the throne, another. (In fact there was a real Macbeth, who had a wife, Gruoch, and they weren't bad people at all.)

I played the part opposite Antony Sher in 1999, at the Swan Theatre in Stratford, the Young Vic in London and the Long Wharf Theatre in New Haven, Connecticut. We also made a film of it for Illuminations Media and Channel 4. I have written quite extensively about the production and the character in *Macbeth* for Faber's *Actors on Shakespeare* series, and again in my book *Brutus and Other Heroines*.

To begin with, the part seemed inaccessible, miles away from me, and I had to spend a lot of time digging into some rather dark territory in my own mind in order to get to her dark heart. Once the show was up and running, I felt pretty solid in understanding her interior thoughts and was very well supported in the production by Antony Sher and the director Greg Doran. I learned that my job was not to judge her but to inhabit the humanity that Shakespeare so brilliantly gives her. I understood that what frightens us in the play is not any 'spirits that tend on mortal thoughts' but the mortal thoughts themselves, the evil that has its source in the human mind.

When we finished playing, I am happy to say I easily shed her cloak. My Lady Macbeth is in the past, but Shakespeare's character will rise again and again.

Having thought and written about her so much I found that my speech for her flowed out of me in a great rush and it fell insistently into two distinct parts, before and after the murder of King Duncan. She becomes almost two different people; the first full of arrogant energy, the second very much chastened.

There is perhaps one thing to point out about this narrative, and that is that the play is full of contradictions as to whether or not the Macbeths have had children together. Lady Macbeth says, 'I have given suck and know how tender 'tis to love the babe that milks me', but Macduff says of Macbeth, 'He has no children', which suggests that whatever child or children they did have perished. Or is Macbeth impotent and Lady Macbeth's child was by another marriage? This would make sense of Macbeth wanting to be rid of Banquo, who the Witches predict will start a dynasty of kings, while Macbeth inherits only a 'barren sceptre and a fruitless crown'. But, just to confuse things, at one point Macbeth says to his wife 'bring forth male children only'. Tony Sher and I were in our late forties when we played the couple, so this line came out as a fit of irrational optimism on Macbeth's part. Everyone who does the play has to take some kind of angle on these contradictions, even if the audience isn't much troubled by them.

For the rest I will let the monologue speak for itself. I imagine Lady M, who spends an awful lot of time alone, first speaking to Macbeth in her head before he comes home from battle and then from some lonely garret in the castle, perhaps as a ghost looking down on her husband as he moves towards his inevitable end.

It Was All Talk

Part I: *Before the Deed*

Oh why should I be stuck *behind* the throne?
You Scottish thanes can't make it on your own.
My witchy sisters had to show the way
(You'd no idea *I* told them what to say).
I met them all upon the blasted heath,
Explained how you had lost your self-belief,
That you were ripe for mischief but too scared
To see your hidden underbelly bared.

With irony they stirred the witches' brew,
But words, not magic, did the work on you.
Don't blame the eye of newt for your ambition,
'Twas your own hunger set you on this mission.
The very mention of the royal role
Began the journey where you lost your soul.
The seed was planted by the witches' toil,
The ground prepared so I could rake the soil.

And oh, if you had planted seed in me
To there take root and breed a dynasty!
But cruel nature ripped my babes away;
Redundant dugs hang lower every day.
I've known the milk of kindness, tasted love,
But it has curdled as some powers above
(Or hell-sent spirits) smote my mother's womb
And turned my fertile body to a tomb.

So now I dare to bargain with those powers
And save our marriage ere it stales and sours.
We're getting old, the tide is at the flood,
So what if we must spill a little blood?
My blood has poured and dried up now. For what?
And you have shed the blood of many a Scot –
Why not a royal Scot? He's old and past it.
You'd make a better king. God damn and blast it.

Part II: *After the Deed*

The deed is done and cannot be unravelled.
No going back, too far we both have travelled.
We have no purpose now, no pact to swear on,
Desire is deadened and the future barren.
These blood-red gloves of mine will ne'er be clean,
It wasn't worth it just to be a queen.

By wide-eyed nightmares all my nerves are frayed
As on to dusty death we jointly wade,
Away from what we purposed at the start.
You soon threw me aside. I'd played my part.
From then our destined paths began to fork:
You followed through where I had been all talk.
I'd *talked* of dashing out a baby's brain –
O hollow boast that spurred a hellish reign! –
Without me you killed Banquo, your best friend,
Then all those pretty chickens met their end,
The offspring of Macduff the Thane of Fife.
Too cowardly yourself to wield the knife,
You hired other hands to do the deed,
So you'd not see his wife and children bleed.

Oh why was I confined behind the throne?
Who knows what might have been had I but known
The terror I'd unleash with all my taunts.
Now I look on from otherworldly haunts,
My candle spent. I can no more engage
But watch you strut and fret upon the stage.

How differently my story could have ended –
If *I'd* been king I'd not have died demented.
I could have ruled with common sense and sanity,
And never made this pact with inhumanity.
But relegated to the role of nagger
I couldn't tell you, 'That is *not* a dagger!
And that is *not* a forest come from Birnam
But human leafy shields and you can't turn 'em
Back to whence they came.' I know it's tough,
But you deserve the vengeance of Macduff.

I say all this with hindsight and with sorrow
While you must face tomorrow and tomorrow . . .
         and tomorrow.

GERTRUDE II

Hamlet

Famously, Gertrude gets one wonderful speech in *Hamlet*, and it is often done as an audition speech for drama schools.

It conjures a romantic picture of Ophelia, a fair maid singing and plucking flowers by the riverbank until she accidentally falls in. Unaware of danger and held up by her full skirts she carries on singing until she is finally dragged down 'to muddy death'. It's an image that has inspired great paintings, most notably that of John Everett Millais.

But recently I was talking to a terrific drama teacher friend, who suggested that Gertrude is prettying up the tragic, ugly suicide of Ophelia in order to soften the blow for her brother Laertes, who has already received the shock of his father's murder and witnessed his sister's madness. Suicide is not romantic, and I thought I would experiment with Gertrude's true upset at the real horror. Suicide may well have crossed Gertrude's own mind, just as it has her son's.

What Gertrude Couldn't Say

You think she died a pretty death? Oh no.
I had to dress it softly for his sake.
A father murdered and a sister lost,
How could I further burden him with truth?
There was no singing nor no flowery bower.
Her bloated corpse was found downstream, impaled
On piercing hawthorn, shredded flesh fish-grey,
Her lips blue-black, her buckled limbs askew,
Bruised and smashed, half naked and mud-caked.
I learned all this from one who happened past,
Who heard her shouted verses coarse and lewd.
'I tried to keep her from that desperate leap
But failed,' quoth he and then began to wail,
'That image will forever burn my brain.'
Poor shepherd punished by our royal acts
With searing sight of ugly suicide,
Untidied, unpoetic, harsh and cruel.
And now 'tis bitter irony to hear
My doctored version spoken as if true
By hopeful students at a drama school;
Or view the image of a red-haired maid
Upheld by floating garments in a stream,
Shrouded by garlands, all inspired by me,
A frozen beauty in a gilded frame.

DARK LADY
SONNET II

Another Dark Lady sonnet. This time I followed the school of thought that the Dark Lady was black or that her father was. In sixteenth-century London there was a small but not insubstantial population of people of African ancestry. Some came over with the Spanish court of Katherine of Aragon and some went far back in history to settlers from the Roman army. Most were working people; some of the women were prostitutes and some were well-connected, having been greeted as curiosities by high society.

In this sonnet, the Lady calls out Shakespeare for romanticising her background. Does he think his readers will only accept her if she is the daughter of an exotic African prince? Her dad was an honest working man born in Shadwell in the East End of London, and what's wrong with that, she asks. Does Shakespeare have to cover up her origins in order to justify his association with her to his courtly friends? Pure speculation of course; Shakespeare doesn't ever discuss her origins in his verses, but I'm interested in the point she makes, and I like her attitude. What follows is something of a retort to the first line of Shakespeare's Sonnet 17, 'Who will believe my verse in time to come.'

My Word Against Yours

Who will believe *my* verse in time to come –
If that my words are ever pressed in print?
Your stronger voice will always strike mine dumb,
My thoughts to powder rendered by your flint.
Who will believe my birth on Shadwell's bank
When you have sailed me in from Afric's shore,
My unknown father of the lowest rank
Erased by fables of a towering Moor?
Ashamed to love a lowborn of my race,
You colour me with false exotic hues,
But 'tis your shame that shames you, not my face,
Despite your weighty talent to a Muse.
Thus I who never lived in foreign climes
Must lie forever in your deathless rhymes.

OLIVIA

Twelfth Night

I played Viola with the RSC back in 1987 and Olivia for BBC Radio even earlier. Having played both parts, I was struck by how entwined they are. The names almost make an anagram, both are in love, neither has a parent around and both are mourning a dead brother. Viola's state of love is infectious. Through her own unrequited love for Orsino she identifies with his unrequited love for Olivia, and her passionate advocacy on his behalf is probably what first turns Olivia on.

I think I am right in remembering that somewhere during the 'willow cabin' speech, when Viola, dressed as the boy Cesario, goes into an ecstatic speech about the willow cabin she would build at her lover's gate, from which she would compose love songs and 'sing them loud even in the dead of night', Deborah Findlay's Olivia turned from being the self-assured commander of a household into a dithering teenager.

It was rather different for me, playing Olivia on radio, mainly because you only get a couple of hours' rehearsal but also because you seldom look into the other actor's eyes. You pour out your heart, whisper your secrets and make love, all to a microphone. The other actor stands by your side with their script held in front of them. In the rehearsal room for a theatre play your script is part shield, part safety net, and the most exciting moment is when you first try playing a scene without it. A script is like those training wheels you had on your first bicycle that helped you get going but were sneakily removed at some point and you find you have been riding a two-wheeler all by yourself. You wobble a bit to begin with and fall over in the gravel and cut your knee, but then you find you can fly. So it is when you make those first tentative steps 'off book' in the rehearsal room and try out those ideas you have been cooking up in your head.

You can look into the other actor's eyes and make a real connection, and by some sort of alchemy you are not Harriet looking into Deborah's eyes but Viola looking into Olivia's eyes, which are looking into Viola's eyes and so the circuit fires on.

Shakespeare's characters are ignorant of what the actors know. Viola doesn't know that Olivia is falling for her (though we later learn that she had clocked some weird starting and fits in her speech), Olivia doesn't realise Cesario is a woman who is in love with Orsino and Viola doesn't realise that her twin brother Sebastian survived the shipwreck and is alive and wandering around in Ilyria.

To me *Twelfth Night* is one of Shakespeare's most perfect plays. He orchestrates the plot so we know just what we need to know when we need to know it, and the comedy comes largely from watching characters who are caught helplessly in a knot that we know he will unravel.

In Act IV, scene 1, Olivia comes face to face with Sebastian, who is conveniently dressed in exactly the same clothes as Cesario, who she supposes him to be. Shakespeare neatly transitions Olivia's awkward love for a woman/boy into a conventionally acceptable love for Sebastian, who the audience is supposed to accept as interchangeable with his twin sister. Sebastian's rescuer, Antonio, is also in love with Sebastian, and the possibility that this love may be requited further complicates the sexual chart.

There are hints of male homosexuality throughout Shakespeare's works but the love between women is always characterised as 'school-days' friendship, childhood innocence' (as per Helena's speech to Hermia in *A Midsummer Night's Dream*), so I thought I would test the idea that Olivia sees through Viola's disguise and is disturbed that she could possibly be falling in love with a woman. I have deliberately emphasised parallel rhythms and echoes with Viola's famous speech 'I left no ring with her . . .'; I have borrowed Shakespeare's words as Olivia likens falling in love to catching the plague; and I have ended, as the original does, with a reckless 'let be!'

Let it Be!

His stance so bold, and yet his voice so light,
Just on the cusp of manhood, perfect place,
That fine hiatus in a person's growing
Before maturity secures their fate.
Her accents soft, her words poetic scorn . . .
Did I say 'her'? How now, what says my heart?
Those blushing peach-skin cheeks more like mine own
Than my dead brother's lately furrèd chin.
Indifferent ruby lips gave her away.
A *sister*-servant to that loathèd lord?
A *sister*-suitor from Orsino's court?
'Good madam, let me see your face' –
So sudden a command, such barefaced brazen.
She had no business with my face, had she?
It was no part of the duke's embassy,
But curiosity beyond her brief
Made her discover what he doted on.
That transitory rapture she betrayed
On seeing my eyes unveiled, I noted then,
'The daylight shines on mine that shadows hers.'
What means this sadness? Why she loves him, sure.
Her boyish suits forbid her to declare
Her passion, so she practises on me!
How will this fadge?
My father had a daughter loved a . . . girl?
It cannot be . . . I rave . . . Beat back my thoughts.
Even so quickly may one catch the plague?
A playful ache to love so hopelessly . . .
Or . . . let my pulse rush freely for this 'swain',

Pursue the wayward love I dare not name.
Concealment is the food of love. Play on!
I'll hang on every word 'Cesario' says,
Though all the world should think I am a le—
Let be! ... (*takes off her ring*) ... Malvolio! I have a
    job for you.

THE MOTHERLESS DAUGHTERS

The Merchant of Venice, A Midsummer Night's Dream, The Tempest, Measure for Measure, Hamlet, As You Like It, The Winter's Tale, King Lear, Titus Andronicus, All's Well That Ends Well, Twelfth Night and Romeo and Juliet

Shakespeare's women usually have a father (dead or alive) who has a big influence on them, but very rarely a mother at their side. Mothers are either dead, separated from the child in infancy (e.g. Hermione/Perdita in *The Winter's Tale* or Thaisa/Marina in *Pericles*), or they are simply not mentioned at all (*King Lear, Twelfth Night* – the list is too long). Perhaps because childbirth was a very dangerous thing (and still can be, of course) many young women in Shakespeare's sphere may have grown up without mothers, or it could be that, for personal reasons, he was never as interested in the mother/daughter relationship as he was in the father/daughter one. For whatever reason, we are left with this frustrating gap in the narrative. I don't entirely blame Shakespeare. Others of his contemporaries fell into the same pattern, and it became – or already was – the template for most fairy stories. The girl without a mother, escaping from a demanding father into the hands of a young protector/prince. The older woman in these stories was usually a wicked stepmother, a witch or occasionally a benign fairy godmother. Guess which I am usually asked to play?

Noting that so many young women in Shakespeare's stories lack a mentoring mother figure and never get to meet one another, I decided to bring them together in a kind of support group, sitting round in a circle sharing their common feelings.

*

Just to remind you of the relevant bits of the plots:

Portia from *The Merchant of Venice*

Portia's father is dead, but made sure he would still control her destiny from beyond the grave. He set a task for any suitor: choose the correct casket, either of gold, silver or lead, and you get to marry her. We watch all the wrong guys go for gold and silver while Bassanio, her chosen love, opts correctly for the lead casket. Portia's sidekick, Nerissa, is confident that fathers know what's best for their daughters even when they are dead:

> Your father was ever virtuous . . . therefore the lottery, that he hath devised . . . whereof who chooses his meaning chooses you, will, no doubt, never be chosen by any rightly but one who shall rightly love.

Hermia from *A Midsummer Night's Dream*

Hermia's dad wants her to marry Demetrius but she wants to marry Lysander. Both boys want to marry her. Dad goes right to the top and asks Theseus, Duke of Athens, to back him up:

> I beg the ancient privilege of Athens,
> As she is mine, I may dispose of her:
> Which shall be either to this gentleman [Demetrius]
> Or to her death.

Theseus reluctantly agrees that Dad has a point and Hermia and Lysander very wisely escape to the forest.

Miranda from *The Tempest*

We never hear about Miranda's mum. She is reared on an island by her father and never meets another human being until she is fifteen, and even then none of them are women.

Isabella from *Measure for Measure*

This poor nun has no parents at all. She does have a brother, but he might be dead by morning.

Ophelia from *Hamlet*

Another one with a controlling father:

OPHELIA:

> I do not know, my lord, what I should think.

POLONIUS:

> Marry, I'll teach you: think yourself a baby.

And a controlling brother:

LAERTES:

> For Hamlet and the trifling of his favour,
> Hold it a fashion and a toy in blood ...
> Then weigh what loss your honour may sustain,
> If with too credent ear you list his songs ...
> Fear it, Ophelia ... Best safety lies in fear:

But no mention of a mother. Gertrude does try to reach out, but she is also trapped behind the lines.

Helena from *A Midsummer Night's Dream*

She is introduced as 'Nedar's daughter' but that is the last we hear of him, which is probably a good thing. One angry father is enough.

Helena loves Demetrius, who doesn't love her – until, that is, he comes under the influence of that little purple flower. At the end of the midsummer night, Puck goes round restoring the lovers' common sense, declaring that 'Jack shall have Jill . . . and all shall be well'. However, he doesn't undo the effects of the potion on Demetrius's eyes.

As she tells us later, Helena is quite glad that Demetrius will remain drugged for the rest of their (we hope) happy life.

Rosalind from *As You Like It*

Rosalind's dad is the Good Duke, who has been banished by her uncle the Bad Duke. She hasn't seen her dad in ages and he doesn't recognise her when she comes across him in the Forest of Arden. He doesn't seem to have missed her much but is happy to see her. He is happy about most things.

Perdita from *The Winter's Tale*

Perdita's mother, Hermione, is the Emperor of Russia's daughter and her father is King Leontes of Sicily, so her sense of being royal isn't far-fetched. If her father had had his way, Perdita would have been murdered in her cot. Instead the lovely Antigonus secreted the babe away from Sicily and left her somewhere in Bohemia. However, he didn't stick around to see she was OK, because he exited pursued by a bear. Instead, some shepherds found her and brought her up. She learned a lot about flowers, as did . . .

Cordelia from *King Lear*

. . . who brings her knowledge of plants and herbs to bear when she meets up with her father King Lear, who is by then mad, sad and naked. She is a warrior, nurse and herbalist all in one. She deserves her own play.

Lavinia from *Titus Andronicus*

This is a very borderline 'joke', but *Titus Andronicus* is a comical/horrific/historical/outlandish play so I felt a little justified. Lavinia is Titus's daughter, who gets her tongue cut out and her hands cut off. This is designed as a punishment for Titus, a defacement of his property. But I suggest it was a lot worse for her.

Helena from *All's Well That Ends Well*

Helena's late father was a doctor, and he was rather a good egg compared to the more aristocratic fathers we have heard about so far. He actually passed something useful on to his daughter, some tricks of the medical trade which she put to good use, curing the King of a weird disease ('a fistula') and then securing the husband of her choice, Bertram, as a reward. So, from beyond the grave, Dad had an indirect hand in Helena's fortune. The fact that Bertram preferred to run into the cannon's mouth than marry Helena rather spoils matters, but the play would be a lot shorter if things had immediately gone her way.

Viola from *Twelfth Night*

Another one with no mother mentioned, a brother she supposes
is dead and an absent father who influences her taste in men.
When the sailor who rescued her from the sea tells her that the
Count Orsino is in charge of the island where she has washed
up, she says, 'Orsino! I have heard my father name him' – so he
must be OK – 'He was a bachelor then,' and immediately her
romantic wheels start whirring.

The fact that Orsino is in love with Olivia until about five
minutes before the curtain call and suddenly switches his af-
fections to the 'boy' Cesario understandably gives Viola pause.

Juliet from *Romeo and Juliet*

Strictly speaking, Juliet does have a mother, but she is not very
hands-on. Her nurse is more of a mother to her, and both will
get a chance to speak later on in this book.

Daddy's Girls

(or Where Are Mothers When You Need Them?)

The setting:

A support group for Motherless Girls with Overbearing Fathers

THESEUS:

> To you your father should be as a god;
> One that composed your beauties, yea, and one
> To whom you are but as a form in wax.

PORTIA FROM BELMONT kicks off the meeting:

> 'Composed our beauties', eh? What, all alone?
> Self-seeded us? Created us by clone?
> Did he, as does the seahorse, solely rear us,
> Assumes therefore the right to overbear us?
> Our mother's part in this remains a mystery,
> So none of us will ever know her history.

HERMIA:

> My daddy went ballistic when I chose
> To land my love Lysander as my spouse.
> He meant Demetrius to be my mate
> And would have forced me to accept this fate
> On pain of death. Defiant, we eloped,
> My chosen one and I, and thus we hoped

To bypass civic laws—

MIRANDA:

                             What's 'sivick' mean?
Forgive me, I'm an otherworldly teen.
My father never mentioned any dam.
Which may account for how naïve I am.
I grew up thinking I was born by magic –
The fact I never knew my ma is tragic.

ISABELLA:

Believe me, child, you're not the only one:
Why else d'you think that I became a nun?

OPHELIA:

I get the convent thing, but I'd miss sex.
Don't tell my dad because he always checks
My every meeting with the moody Dane.
It makes me so embarrassed . . .

HELENA OF ATHENS *(mumbles)*:

                             Don't complain.
Try being me! No father in the show:
Who's Nedar anyway? I'd love to know.

ROSALIND:

Like all of you, my mum I don't recall
And Dad in exile seems to be in thrall

To nature now and lives out in the wild.
He's probably forgotten I'm his child.
He's totally absorbed in this adventure.
Despite all that, I love him *in absentia*.

PERDITA:

I *have* a mother back in Sicily . . .
(*The other girls look up*)
But 'cos my father treated her so pissily
Her loyal servants figured out a plot,
Told Dad she'd died but actually she'd not.
They brought me to Bohemia to be reared
While Mum lives still (in statue form, I heard).
I was so young, I don't remember her,
But have the vaguest memory of a . . . bear?
Kind summer trees caress me with their leaves
And sheep lend me their fleece on winter eves.
But somewhere in my depths there's always been
A sense that I'm the daughter of a queen.

HELENA OF ATHENS:

Well hark at you! Expect us all to kneel, yeah?
Let's hear it from a *real* princess. Cordelia?

CORDELIA:

I find it hard to talk about this stuff,
Can't seem to heave my feelings to my mouth.

HELENA OF ATHENS:

> How about you, Lavinia?
> (*silence*)
> Lavinia?
> (*silence*)
> Never mind.

All the girls race to embrace Lavinia.

PORTIA FROM BELMONT (*changing the atmosphere*):

> Dead fathers are no better, take my word:
> I swear my situation is absurd.
> My father laid the law down with a quiz,
> Beyond the grave made sure that I was his.
> My suitors had to guess: Gold? Silver? Lead?
> And till they got it right I couldn't wed.
> So by this cryptic game he keeps control
> Until some husband earns the owner's role.

HELENA OF ROUSSILLON:

> So, indirectly, was *my* life controlled,
> My father posthumously kept his hold.
> A stateless orphan into service hired,
> I had to keep my place or I'd be fired.
> I loved my mistress's son the gorgeous Bertram,
> But he could never see beyond my serfdom.
> I found a way to 'scape my lowly station –
> No prizes if you guess my inspiration.
> You're right: my dad, a doctor by whose skill,
> Transferred to me, I cured the King when ill.

The King was housing Bertram as his ward,
Gave him to me to wed as my reward.
'Twas meant as thanks that I had saved his life,
But Bertie didn't want me as a wife.

VIOLA:

I hadn't really thought, but now I see
'The wife unwanted' could apply to me.
So also could the theme of distant Pa,
Perpetuating power from lands afar.
Soon after I was shipwrecked in Ilyria
Began my sad delusion and deliria.
That Dad knew Count Orsino spurred the thought
Of dressing up and working at his court.
From that mad move my lovesickness began.
I loved that father figure man to man.
It's complicated. Doting left me dumb,
'Twas then of all times that I missed a mum.
She might have helped the problem to untangle,
At least approached it from a different angle.
As usual, in Act Five Will tied the knot,
All hitched and mismatched for a tidy plot.

HELENA OF ATHENS:

Well I'm quite grateful for Will's lazy writing,
For letting ends hang loose and expediting
Triple weddings and a final dance.
His vagueness gives our married life a chance.
He wrapped things up so Jack could have his Jill,
But my Demetrius is spellbound still.

He sees me through perpetual purple haze.
I only hope this isn't just a phase.

CORDELIA:

If ever he wakes up, I have the potion
That can revive his amorous devotion.
Rank fumiter and darnel, cuckoo-flowers,
Will keep him stiff with ecstasy for hours.

JULIET:

But careful with the timing once you're dosed,
We got it slightly wrong and now we're toast.

TUTTE:

So hear us, future writers, when we say,
'We need our mums, SO PUT THEM IN THE PLAY.'

LADY CAPULET

Romeo and Juliet

S hakespeare's son Hamnet died in 1596, aged eleven. *Romeo and Juliet* is said to have been written between 1594 and 1596, so we can't know for sure whether Hamnet's death had happened or was yet to happen when Shakespeare wrote the play. If he didn't already, he was soon to know first-hand the terrible grief of losing a young child. With or without this personal insight, his psychological genius was such that he knew what words to give to his characters in order to wrestle with and tame such a grief.

In a play written only a short while after *Romeo and Juliet* (*King John*, 1596–7) he has Constance describe how:

> Grief fills the room up of my absent child,
> Lies in his bed, walks up and down with me,
> Puts on his pretty looks, repeats his words,
> Remembers me of all his gracious parts,
> Stuffs out his vacant garments with his form;
> Then, have I reason to be fond of grief?

(Unforgettably beautiful – how I wish that play was done more often, if only to give that role of Constance to a hungry actress.)

Then, much later (around 1605–6) there is Lear with his agonising:

No, no, no life!
Why should a dog, a horse, a rat, have life,
And thou no breath at all? Thou'lt come no more,
Never, never, never, never, never!

I can't help wanting to know more of what Lady Capulet is going through when she sees her daughter lying in the family vault. Shakespeare gives her just two lines:

O me! This sight of death is as a bell,
That warns my old age to a sepulchre.

Dramaturgically I understand that the very starkness of the end of the play imprints the tragedy on us more effectively than would a series of wailing eulogies, but still. Lady Capulet is that rare thing in Shakespeare's canon, a young woman's mother. For a mother, the death of a child that she has carried in her womb is a different kind of wrench than for a father. Shakespeare gives little space for that in *Romeo and Juliet*. He saves it up for Constance.

During the play, Lady Capulet is upstaged by her ranting husband and the cosy, comical Nurse. What we do know is that she was about the same age as Juliet when she married. It was customary to marry off high-born girls early for breeding purposes, so I was curious to invent a bit of Lady C's backstory and add that into the context of the play.

A Mother's Grief

I don't have many words, am seldom seen
And yet I am the *centre* of *my* play.
I too was made to marry at thirteen,
Forced into motherhood without delay.

Old Capulet he couldn't wait to start
So I was ploughed and plundered, split and torn,
My fragile frame untimely ripped apart,
And thus my lovely Juliet was born.

So weak and frail, myself could make no milk,
Passed mewling infant into Nurse's care,
My aching body laced once more in silk
And whalebone ribs suppressing my despair.

I bore her but could never feed or own her,
From unfamiliar babe was kept away,
Led by my lord through houses of Verona
As trophy bride and mother on display.

With time I learnt to 'scape with loosened laces,
To watch my cygnet daughter grow in beauty.
Sweet gossiping in nursery oasis
Was wondrous rare relief from wifely duty.

Too quick my Juliet grew to nubile age.
Pre-emptively my sister-friendship froze,
I shut my daughter out and closed a page,
And found a fitting prince to pluck my rose.

I had no choice, I knew of nothing other,
Only the rules and duties of an heiress,
From me to Juliet passed as from *my* mother.
At least, I thought, she'll always have her Paris ...

But now she'll never more come back to me.
Too high a price for laying down of swords.
Two mothers both alike in agony
Embrace cold stone, too late, too deep for words.

THE NURSE

Romeo and Juliet

Juliet gave me my break into radio drama because aged about thirty I sounded thirteen. It was the first and only time my childish voice came in handy, when the BBC cast me as Juliet alongside Bill Nighy as Mercutio and the brilliant Elizabeth Spriggs as the Nurse. Liz was bliss to play opposite. Usually in radio drama, you stand side by side and speak into a microphone holding your script like a barrier in front of you. Other actors drift in and out of the corner of your eye and, like it says on the tin, we perform on air with nothing but our breath and our voices to play with. In contrast to all that, Liz felt solid, in the room with me, a well-cushioned shoulder to cry on – I did quite a lot of that – and a brilliant example of comic timing.

I think the first Shakespeare play I ever saw was *Romeo and Juliet*, with Judi Dench playing Juliet and one Peggy Mount playing the Nurse. I was very young and hardly understood it, but what I do remember was both of these actresses' voices. We all know what Judi Dench sounds like and can imagine how that unique timbre would have stayed with a child. Peggy Mount is probably only remembered by very few people reading this, but she had a fierce, almost manly voice, and because of this usually played comic stalwarts – the harridan wife or the barking matron. She was 'no beauty', as they say, and like all actors she was cast according to her voice and appearance. I am convinced her looks belied her and that there was a soft and serious person underneath.

She was perfect for Juliet's nurse, who has also been typecast. She is the clown with the heart of gold who becomes a turncoat at the end when she encourages Juliet to forget Romeo and marry Paris.

So here I want to dig below the comic surface and let her tell her side of the story. We know only that she has cared for the thirteen-year-old Juliet since infancy, and that she had her own daughter Susan, but

> Susan and she – God rest all Christian souls! –
> Were of an age: well, Susan is with God;
> She was too good for me:

How does she view the Capulets? What is it like to breastfeed a baby that is not yours? To have lost your own daughter and then have a second 'daughter' taken out of your hands?

Another Mother's Grief

But first a revelation:
You think I'm all 'Oddsboddikins!' and 'Lordie!'
A 'Lawksamercy!' slap-and-tickle fool,
Old saws, wives' tales and country cunning bawdy,
But silly souls have deeper feelings too.

My ladybird, my lammikin, my own –
Well, not quite mine, but more of mine than hers –
My Lady Scarce a stranger, cool as stone,
Her mother's milk a dribbled, curdled curse.
My own breasts teemed with juice enough for two,
Juliet and Susan suckling either side.
Sweet playful stems to lovely blossoms grew
'Til fever claimed my Susan and she died.
Poured all my tears and love in Juliet's way
Within the womb-like safety of our nursery.
Her parents' swooping visits, once a day,
Were formal things, unnerving and quite cursory.
For so it is in families of quality
A girl-child is for breeding, not for knowing.
It's pedigree that counts with the nobility:
Some spineless scion needs her for his sowing.
So when my J. met R. I was delirious,
A rebel child at last to break the mould.
The unsmooth course of love however perilous
Can carve new fissures in the walls of old.
But then – Oh curse my cowardly compliance! –
When things looked bleak I let my darling down,
Encouraged her to go for the alliance

With Mr Safe-and-Bland, that bit-part clown.
And now the pain! I'll never be forgiven.
My ancient limbs must ever bear my fault.
All labours lost as she to death was driven,
Oh fatal loins that led to such a vault!

Postscript from The Nurse

This was prompted by the fact that the famous 'balcony scene' where Romeo and Juliet meet privately after the masked ball is somewhat misnamed. Shakespeare only tells us that 'Juliet appears above at a window'. She sighs to herself, 'Ay me!' Romeo's response inspired the title of this book – 'She speaks: O, speak again, bright angel!' – and the most romantic scene in literature takes off.

A Correction

I see why Mr Shakespeare took this story:
To show the healing power of lovers' alchemy,
Two stars forever staged in tragic glory –
Although he never specified a balcony.

ARIEL

The Tempest

I n 2016, I played Prospero in *The Tempest*, which was the third play in the all-female Shakespeare Trilogy conceived and directed by Phyllida Lloyd for London's Donmar Warehouse. Radically, she chose to set the plays in a women's prison and to cast only women. The project started from an impulse to address the imbalance of male and female roles in Shakespeare and the consequent advantage male actors had over female actors in terms of experience and exercise of their talent. But over the five years of developing and playing them, the productions became something more.

It was not just a narrow band of women actors who were under-represented in Shakespearean cast lists but many different *types* of women – women of different ages, appearances, ethnicities and classes. By setting the plays in a prison, the casting net was thrown very wide and this new non-conformity became key to our reasons for performing the plays. Audiences that identified with the people they saw on stage felt a new kind of connection with these four-hundred-year-old plays, as did countless young people and students. The trilogy grew to be as much about this inclusivity and diversity as about the plays themselves. They gave people both on- and off-stage access to one of the central pillars of Western language and culture, and access to the poet of all of our humanity. On a personal level, I felt I was sharing my love of Shakespeare with a much wider world.

It rather pleases me to think I probably don't have to explain here what needed so much justification back in 2012, when we began the work, since now cross-gender and cross-racial casting is (almost) an accepted norm.

Phyllida picked her cast, many of whom had never spoken a word of Shakespeare, because of their inherent intelligence, musicality, their willingness to learn and fit into an ensemble and bring something unusual to it. Thanks to her and the work we did, those actors quickly took up the reins and made Shakespeare their own, part of their actor's equipment, with lasting effect.

In *Brutus and Other Heroines* I described a lot of the process of developing the first two plays: *Julius Caesar*, in which I played Brutus, and *Henry IV*, in which I played Henry, but I hadn't yet started rehearsing *The Tempest* by the time the book went to print. In those first two characters I focused on what it might be like to be a man, to have to make major political decisions and to take responsibility for a nation, while also dealing with domestic relationships with a wife or a son. I strode about in army greatcoats and flak jackets, and sat with my legs spread wide. The physicality affected us all in a similar way; it liberated us from any self-conscious vanity. We felt the permission to take up space and own it.

For Prospero, things were different. We struggled to find an outward appearance for this 'magician'. Pointy hats and star-spangled cloaks were out, so what to do instead?

Even in the dress rehearsal I had no answer, and in a fit of pique I burst out, 'I don't have a costume and we open in a few days!' Phyllida looked at me as I perched in a tennis umpire's chair, looking down on the scene, and she said, '*That's* your costume.' I was wearing the prison grey tracksuit bottoms we all wore, and a sleeveless white T-shirt that didn't hide my female shape. From then on, Prospero's gender was immaterial, and a significant consequence of that was that s/he became one of the parts in which I felt closest to myself.

The same undefined gender applies to Ariel (in our production played by an androgynous Jade Anouka) and I felt Ariel could belong in this collection alongside other female voices as 'they'.

Shakespeare so often plays with theatre metaphors when describing human life, and his Sonnet 23 'As an unperfect actor on the stage' inspired the first line of this Ariel sonnet (though there is no other link in meaning). We often think of Ariel as the mind, the spirit of the creator – Prospero's and Shakespeare's creation who has very little genuine autonomy. Ariel is a servant of the poet, and both loves and hates that position. Ariel is fearful that without the creator they may be nothing but air. I think actors, myself included, recognise that sense of lack of self from time to time. So this is a poem about actors as much as it is about Ariel.

Ariel's Sonnet

Much as an actor hides behind a role
Avoiding capture, so I shift my shape.
A paradox who's never truly whole,
Belonging nowhere, longing to escape.
I wear a coat of other people's skins,
Clap on the helmet of my master's thoughts
Not sure where his path ends or mine begins,
An aerial pet performing somersaults.
I zip around the island, flame the sea,
Dive deep inside the core of spinning Earth,
Paint music in the air where thought is free,
But love doth make me ask 'What's freedom worth?'
Unchained from him who loves me, I do fear
That loosed to viewless winds I'll disappear.

CALIBAN

The Tempest

Caliban the 'monster' is one of those characters, rather like the Witches in *Macbeth*, who modern directors find hard to locate in a contemporary context. Shakespeare's audience certainly believed in witchcraft and probably believed that faraway islands harboured strange half-human creatures. Nowadays we have to go to the bottom of the sea to see extraordinary unimagined beasts, or we invent them from outer space. Different productions have used the character of Caliban to make many different metaphysical, psychological or political points. He is portrayed as our animal nature, our untameable antisocial dark side, our insanity, our criminality – or we have excused him as a victim, a slave of colonialism.

These days we rightly tread carefully around the portrayal of monsters. We recognise what constitutes a human being and abhor any society that labels people as 'subhuman', 'monstrous' or 'freaks'. But Shakespeare did intend Caliban to be both scary and comic in ways that can be hard for us to go along with.

Whichever way you cut it, Caliban *is* something different from the other humans in the play. He is the son of Sycorax, the local witch; he is spurned by Prospero because he tried to rape his daughter, Miranda; and, learning that, the audience is repelled by him. They are also somewhat threatened by his vengeful anger against Prospero, who owns him like a slave, and next we pity him when Prospero threatens him with diseases and punishments, denying him any freedom from burdensome work. But having set this creature up as repulsive, scary and pitiable, for the rest of the play he is the butt of jokes – and not very funny ones at that. Stefano the drunk and Trinculo the clown harness 'the monster's' rage and use him in their absurd plot to kill Prospero and make Stefano king of the island.

I felt Caliban belonged in this book of female voices perhaps because, as with Ariel, I cannot shake the image of them as women in a prison. In our version, Caliban was played by Sophie Stanton, who managed to embrace the anomaly of clown and would-be rapist.

At the end of Shakespeare's play, Ariel is released and all the characters (including Prospero) return to Naples to resume life in a patriarchal society. Prospero's titles are restored and Miranda will become Queen of Naples. Caliban is sort of forgiven, but we presume he stays behind on the island. Shakespeare's audience (and many in later ages) expected a happy ending in his comedies, with all the ends tied up.

Nowadays we need something that better reflects the unresolved, open-ended world we experience, and don't trust neat resolutions.

So, in our version, going back to Naples meant being released from prison. Prospero (or Hannah, as my prisoner was named) was in prison for life. One by one the cast of prisoners, dressed in their home clothes, say goodbye to me, and as I settle back on my rough-blanketed iron bed, the prisoner cast as Caliban wordlessly runs the floor-cleaner over my cell floor. She too is in it for life but, like the two characters in the play, we are never truly reconciled to one another. For all the shedding of worldly ties and preparedness for death, Caliban remains an unsettled, unsettling thorn in Prospero's/Hannah's side.

As with other voices in this book, I want to explore Caliban's inner life. This person is an outcast, full of self-hatred and malice mostly due to the cruelty with which they have been treated all their life, but they also have one beautiful and famous speech, which begins 'Be not afeard; the isle is full of noises'. That sensitivity to beauty and longing for escape into dreams surprises and confuses us. A stroke of Shakespearean genius.

Caliban's Secret

Ugly Mugly, never Cuddly,
I blot the page with rot and rage.
I welcome stones that hurt my bones,
Jagged boulders, buckled shoulders.
Engendered in a dog-piss ditch,
Ungendered offspring of a witch,
Nor fish nor filly, cock nor colt,
Spat from the womb to cause revolt,
Unholy mix of scales and feathers
I look for mates but know no others.
No name to tell me who I am,
Till He came up with 'Caliban'.

Banned from humanity, but by Him tamed;
Tutored and tortured with the self-same hand,
Wrangled with whips – but what's the carrot?
This barren bogland to inherit?
Will books and language set me free?
No! Monster always let me be.
In slop-pail slurry let me lie,
Pig-malion alien in my sty.
I'll pester blest Miranda with my stench.
If you invent me, shall I not revenge?
You taught me words so I shall spit and spout,
Delight in dancing all the poison out:
(*singing and dancing*)
Stamping, stomping, rudely romping,
Ban, ban Caliban!
I sicken Sycorax,

Prospero impostero ...
(*comes to a standstill*)
You set the Spirit free while I am bound
Forever in my cave, or so You thought.
But in my ear sweet noises softly sound,
A music no magician ever taught.
Beyond, above, below and everywhere
The buzz of wings and zephyrs in the air
Lulls me to sleep where no one reaches me,
And in that sleep how lovely I can be.

MIRANDA

The Tempest

Miranda is the magician Prospero's daughter. I am sad to say I never played her as I rather love her, but by the time I was up and running as a Shakespearean actor I was way too old.

Miranda is an unspoilt, almost feral creature, untrained in the ways of civilisation other than the paternalist patterns that Prospero inevitably brings with him in his exile from Milan and repeats in his teaching of her.

When he conjures the storm that lands his enemies on the shores of the island, he sees many opportunities, one of which is to make Miranda fall in love with and marry the King's son Ferdinand, so that she will eventually be Queen of Naples.

Miranda has never seen other humans until the shipwreck throws this group on to the island's sands. She famously gasps in wonder when she first sees them all, saying, 'O brave new world, / That has such people in't!'

The journey of the character reminds me of mine and so many young girls' journeys from tomboy freedom to ladylike decorum and conformity, where we lose so much of that un-selfconscious daring and spend a lot of time later in life trying to retrieve it.

In our all-female production for the Donmar Shakespeare Trilogy, Miranda never did quite conform. Leah Harvey played Miranda and Sheila Atim was Ferdinand; their gender was immaterial. At their wedding both bride and groom wore a combination of tutus and top hats, tail coats and necklaces never assigned to one or other gender.

In one way Miranda is totally imprinted by a man's teachings and at the end of the play she is left to fit in to the existing masculine hierarchy of Shakespeare's world. She is an innocent, but Shakespeare also gives her a lively, brilliant mind that *could* question and resist his own and Prospero's plans for her. She also has a unique imagination, fuelled by her unique upbringing.

In this piece I wanted to explore free-associating verse to mirror her lack of formal training. I speculate on Miranda's private musings about her own situation and her ability to imagine a far distant future, a future where she catches up with us.

Sandwriting

Freefalling words
freewheeling
the whee free from feeling
free the verse
from the five-beat pent-up pentameter
from the great I-AM-bic.
No more 'I am'
Just Me.

Abandoned Miranda
lives with abandon.
Who named me Miracle?
Must have been her,
my longed-for long-dead mother.
Or was I birthed by the sea
like Aphrodite
Her-ma-aphrodite?
Is that what I am?
No more 'I am'
just Me.

So confused

I DIDN'T ASK TO BE CONJURED

'Fifteen years ago' s/he tells me I was born –
my father/author/only parent Prospeare –
clean and pink as a kitten's yawn
a blank page unwritten.

The unruly shoreline was my school
shell knowledge with an ever-wiping slate.
With my lap full of fish, I sat, the wavelets slapping
– my only applause.
My nails dug in the mud and sand for crabs.
My teeth ripped flesh off fish and fowl,
sucked juice from beetle carcasses,
chased hogs and hares and hornèd things,
could light a fire or hold my breath to reach the
        ocean bed
full fathom five . . . (well maybe not so far).

By the way, that thing about drowning his/her book . . .
S/he says that all the time.
The seabed is littered with broken staffs and
        drownèd books.
Sometimes they drift up to the shore –
Littoral literature.
'You're too clever by half,' s/he tells me
but what else am I to do with only time on my hands
and nothing to play with but words and sand?

From Prospero I learnt an alphabet
learnt to count times and distances,
roast food, make tools, ease his troubled dreams.
In his sleep he talks of Milan –
as if it were a place outside
away, beyond, behind him in the past.
He doesn't seem to see the ILL-ness is inside.
The Isle is in the M-AN

But I do remember a journey –
salt spray, salt tears and a leaky bark

Then noises and sweet air and
welcome calm as we lay hollowed out
on the pillowy shore

Soon Parent thrashed rushes, cut down trees,
diverted waters tamed all creatures of the isle
for me, s/he said.

Gave me the monster as a toy.
Reared us together,
Too busy conjuring to notice
the spongey mounds sprouting on my front,
how I abhorred the pawing prodigy
who grabbed me round my stalk
and squeezed the childhood out of me.

But now! This storm!
Not in *my* name!
People screaming hair on fire
dragged into the mire.
Not in *my* name.

While Ariel, the air apparent,
does our parent's bidding
spins the waves into chaos,
I, not trained in heartlessness,
pity the creatures spilt into the foam,
brave sad beings
sodden with histories,
new sights for me.

And O, the beauty
of log-burdened Ferdinand!

So what if my Maker engineered it all
to avenge and arrange my marriage?
Queen of Naples?
Not in *my* name.

Now I understand . . .
Ferdinand
is just the
Bird in Hand
There may be others in the world out there!

Now my dreams are Peopled.
I see towering gods and giant silver fish
flying to connecting lands
and smaller gods, not flesh and blood like me,
that replicate the creatures, speak in monotones,
do chores like Caliban. But some
begin to use their powers too much
and force the creatures to lay down their tools
and drown their books, and split their staffs
redundant, sad and powerless.
What then? I wake.
My maker Shakespeare threading through my thoughts
'Human Intelligence is not artifice, say I'
(Say that out loud and you will hear my rhyme)
To hope a thing can make it true, it seems.
Oh brave new world that makes the stuff of dreams.

ANNE HATHAWAY

Shakespeare's Wife

N ow that we are increasingly taking an interest in the muses, wives and daughters of great artists and hoping to recover talents that history has missed through a traditional lack of interest in women's lives, I wonder about Anne Hathaway. What can it have been like to be married to Shakespeare?

I wonder whether she saw anything special in the pimply Warwickshire youth who got her pregnant, and whether he left her completely behind from early in their marriage, or perhaps she developed with him. Maybe she had a hand in his work or maybe she took no interest in it at all. Was she his downtrodden 'clog'* or beloved helpmeet?

Did the death of their son Hamnet bring them closer together or were they separated by their individual griefs?

How did she spend those many months when Shakespeare was following his muse, courting fame and earning a good living in London? Did she wait patiently for him, engrossed in domestic duties, or did she make the most of her own freedom?

What were those last five years of his life like, when he had left the stage and settled down as a Stratford burgher? Did she have any notion of the scale of her husband's genius and immortality?

---

* Shakespeare's word for a wife who weighs her husband down, holds him back from freedom ('Here comes my clog' is Bertram's aside, describing his newly betrothed Helena to his friend Parolles in *All's Well That Ends Well*).

Frustratingly, we will never know unless some correspondence between them comes to light. Quite a few of Shakespeare's sonnets could be interpreted as referring affectionately to his wife, though that reading is not generally put forward. It seems many people prefer to take the more cynical or misogynist view that Shakespeare couldn't wait to get away from Anne and hit the lights of London with all the sexual temptations it could offer.

There are so many lines of enquiry I am tempted to follow, but with so little evidence I am necessarily stuck with inadequate speculations. I narrowed them down to four in four sonnets written at different stages of her life. I am of course presuming that Anne had learned to write. Perhaps her husband taught her.

Anne's Sonnet I is somewhat coloured by Shakespeare's Sonnet 138, 'When my love swears that she is made of truth'.

Sonnet II was inspired by Carol Ann Duffy's poem 'Anne Hathaway' in *The World's Wife*. The poem revises the significance of the 'second-best bed' which Shakespeare famously left to Anne in his will. It had long been interpreted as a slighting of Anne, but Duffy picks up on the fact that the best bed was used for guests while the second-best bed would have been the marital one with all its intimate memories.

For Sonnet III, I imagined a connection between William and Anne's grief for their son Hamnet and Constance's wonderful speech in *King John* about her dead child Arthur, which I refer to earlier in the section on Lady Capulet.

And for Sonnet IV, I dared to speculate that Shakespeare might have a personal reason to know what Emilia was talking about when, at the end of Act IV of *Othello*, she tells Desdemona:

> Let husbands know
> Their wives have sense like them: they see and smell
> And have their palates both for sweet and sour,

As husbands have . . .
Then let them use us well: else let them know,
The ills we do, their ills instruct us so

Anne's Sonnets

Sonnet I

Another View

Those who'd have him hate me have maligned
A partnership that thrived on telling truth.
He chased me first while I for months declined
The kisses of a foolish fumbling youth.
I grant he spoke uncommon well, but know
The breath that whispered honeyed words was foul.
The beard upon his chin was slow to grow
('Tho later it would serve to hide his jowl),
His locks too soon gave way to egg-shell pate
Which others praised as proof of gravitas –
They seldom saw the fool whom I'd berate
For boring me *in vino veritas.*
He'd call me fool but knew that when it mattered
I'd tell him true where some false courtier flattered.

Sonnet II

Anne's Pledge

Let me not to the coinage of new words admit
    impediment,
Nor block the writer's urge to share his dreams:
This marriage to the Bard is an experiment,
A partnership more equal than it seems.
Let me accommodate the Poet's muse
And house his weary body when he's here.
All careless, cold behaviour I'll excuse:
His art shall be *my* art and lifelong care.
Let people think I shackle him and chain him,
A dull and rustic housewife, second-best.
They'll never feel the sheets that we have lain in,
The lasting love that is his *true* bequest.
For though he be the Poet for All Time
The name he coined for *me* is only mine.

Sonnet III

Hamnet

Can I describe the colour of his skin,
The lock of dampened hair upon his brow,
The struggling pulse, the limbs so small and thin –
That questing look that haunts me even now?
My husband might, but cannot lift his pen –
The poet-playwright sunk in wordless gloom.
In double hell we cannot share our pain
So grief hangs silent in our dead child's room.
My ghost-boy beckons me where'er I go,
Lies in my bed, walks with me when I wake,
The sweet one who the world will never know.
I beg my husband 'Write, for pity's sake!
Let Hamnet's name survive us in some fashion,
But in a fiction, in a dream of passion.'

Sonnet IV

Anne Confesses

When Will departs to London's city streets
It gives me time to study and to edit
His sonnets where the theme too oft repeats,
Improve them, though I never get the credit.
While he besports himself in Lady's chamber
Or flirts with My Lord This or Master That
He bade me sign, in secret, a disclaimer
To never from the bag release the cat.
This bargain seems quite fair to me on balance,
I couldn't match his genius if I tried.
Besides correcting verse I've other talents
Which I can put to use where I reside.
So while with London loves he's misbehavin'
I copy his example by the Avon.

PROSPERO'S PRONOUNS

A Postscript

Prospero is often understood to be a version of Shakespeare himself. The inventor, the controller and creator of imaginary worlds who is at the same time human and subject to the laws of the real world. When I played the part for the Donmar Shakespeare Trilogy, very occasionally while I was delivering Prospero's speech renouncing his powers, drowning his book and breaking his staff, I felt an overwhelming sadness, almost as if I were inside Shakespeare's head as he prepared to lay down his pen and retire to Stratford. In those moments I had an intimation of my own much less consequential bowing-out, which inevitably lay in wait.

I found myself in quite a new place, neither man nor woman but person; an ageing person, someone who has to learn to let go. Prospero has to let go of past grudges, his anger, his authority. He has to loosen the ties of love and let his daughter go her own way. I don't have children, but I related to this preparation for the next and last stage of life, and I was moved and excited to, as it were, hand over the baton to a new generation of actors.

Letting go began to feel good. Shedding the outer casing of gender felt good. Playing Prospero put me in touch with a kind of inner essence of Me and the ungraspable fact that that Me will also have to be renounced at some point.

Most of us for most of the time experience ourselves as I or Me. It is only when we interact with others that our age, gender and ethnicity have any relevance. I don't wake up in the morning thinking, *I am an old woman*. In the boundless regions inside our own heads we can drop all our labels. I have always been tantalised by the gap between a person's inner thoughts and their outer 'message'.

I respect the needs of some people to remove what they see as confining definitions and use their chosen pronouns, but perhaps the most important pronoun is the unifying We. For good or bad – and all the middle territory between – we are in this thing together. Good to remember the humbling perspective of Shakespeare/Prospero:

> . . . We are such stuff
> As dreams are made on, and our little life
> Is rounded with a sleep.

Acknowledgements

Where to begin with acknowledgements and thanks?

The obvious frontrunner is William Shakespeare himself, who invented all the wonderful characters I've played and been playing with, and without whom my life would have been so different.

Then in some kind of chronological order: the Coram Shakespeare Schools Foundation, who inadvertently kicked off this journey with their What You Will competition in which they invited young people to create a new speech for a character in a Shakespeare play. They asked me, as a patron, to invent something myself as an example so I wrote 'What Gertrude *Wanted* to Say' to see if that might start the challenge. I have no idea whether or not I inspired anybody, but I enjoyed the exercise so much that I wrote a few more and then a few more.

I soon started trying them out on people and I thank the following infinitely for their encouragement and tips and corrections to my early attempts: Greg Doran, Kate Littlewood, Juliet Stevenson, Phyllida Lloyd, Kate Pakenham, Daisy Boulton, Noma Dumezweni, Rachael Stirling, Claire van Kampen, Mark Rylance, Paul Edmondson, John Caird, Francesca Gardiner, my brilliant writer friends at Randomwood, Jen Joseph and friends at Clean Break who were such great sounding boards, Penny Cherns for inspiring 'Gertrude II', the late, loved Peter Wilson for giving me his blessing shortly before his death, my friend and erstwhile agent Faith Evans, who got me to write in the first place back in the 1990s, and my new agent Caroline Michel for her wonderful enthusiasm for the idea of this book from the moment we met. Thanks also to Francesca Morgan and Kieron Fairweather at PFD for their keen feedback early on.

Lennie Goodings has been involved in my writing life for at least a decade, patiently prodding for a new book from me and allowing me to try out ideas and false starts. When the idea for *She Speaks!* came up it just seemed to fit perfectly with Virago and I have been blessed by Lennie's kindness, her sharp mind and the gift of her accumulated wisdom. I have loved working with the whole Virago/Little, Brown team, those who met and greeted me – Sarah Savitt, Jess Purdue and Louise Harvey – and those I haven't met but who have contributed to the publication behind the scenes.

Zoe Gullen never wavered through all my nit-picking and last minute cries of 'oh, I have a better idea' during the copy-editing process. Thanks to Zoe for her tact and great suggestions. Thanks to Susan de Soissons for her faith in promoting the book. My gratitude also to cover designer Nico Taylor for his generous collaboration with my goddaughter Kaye Blegvad, whose illustrations so wittily complement the verses and help to set the tone.

Thanks to Mika Kasuga for so speedily taking the book up and to all the Union Square team for the USA publication.

I know everyone says this, but I truly could not have done this without my husband Guy Paul. He kept me fed and watered while I was trying to fit the writing into my acting schedule. He is a brilliant rhymester in his own right and I have been astonished by his insight, his generosity and his patience while I tried out each half-baked poem on him long before they were ready to be heard.

Caterina Petruchiana

Octavia Menor

Anne Neville

Cressida Ubiquita Desdemon

ivia of Itivia

Sister J

Susanna Capulet